FOR OTHER GHOSTS

For Other Ghosts

First Edition

Published by Awst Press
P.O. Box 49163
Austin, TX 78765

awst-press.com
awst@awst-press.org

Printed in the United States of America
Distributed by Small Press Distribution

ISBN: 978-0-9971938-7-9
Library of Congress Control Number: 2018952769

Cover illustration by Maggie Chiang
Editing by Tatiana Ryckman
Copyediting by Emily Roberts
Book design by LK James

To the Circle,

To the Family,

To P.J.,

For all the reasons.

"Our world, the world of each one of us, is not a totum revolutum, but is organized in 'pragmatic fields.' Each thing belongs to one or more of these fields, in which it interlinks its being-for with that of others, and so on successively."

José Ortega y Gasset *(Man and People)*

Translated by William R. Trask

CONTENTS

FOR OTHER GHOSTS

DONALD QUIST

THEIRS & MINE

THEY WOULD BE WAITING

The engine rumbled, running idle. Our driver tried to explain the situation to the soldier. Simple math: fourteen people crammed into a twelve-passenger church van, the funeral party, and two more in the truck behind us, three if counting the body. We had reached a civilian checkpoint on the way to Atiavi, where my grandmother was born and would be buried. I was crowded in the back row between Cousin Junior and Auntie Edna, watching my father in the seat in front of me as sweat beaded on the crown of his shaved head. I wrote it down in the journal in my lap and imagined what he might be thinking.

My father would have noticed the defensiveness in the driver's voice. My father drove a cab in America. Most of his fares avoided conversation, allowing him to listen as they chatted on their cell phones or to other passengers. He listened to them laugh with friends and family. He listened to them lie to lovers and even to themselves. Years of overhearing had taught him about tone and inflection. He was always listening, especially at that moment. I'm sure of it. He could hear the undertones, a tremble in the driver's voice that mimicked the quiver of the van.

"Sir, earlier we went through a security roadblock and were cleared to pass. We are coming from a funeral in Accra."

"And where are you heading?" the soldier asked.

"The burial is in a small fishing village on the Keta Lagoon."

"So you all are not smugglers then?" The soldier grinned.

"No, sir," the driver said.

The road led to the border of Togo and was often used by bandits to traffic stolen goods in and out of Ghana. Military personnel were stationed every fifty miles to screen vehicles. Our driver was not a smuggler, but my father could tell he was nervous around these army men.

"Do you have a license?" the soldier said.

The driver retrieved a small plastic card from his pocket.

The soldier read over it. He flipped it in his hand from one side to the other, back and forth and then back again. "Are you sure this license was issued to you by the Driver and Vehicle Licensing Authority?"

"Yes," the driver said.

The soldier held out a finger. He walked around the front of the vehicle to the side of the road. Off the right shoulder of the motorway two officers sat on a bench beneath a small four-post shelter with a thatched roof and a single tin wall spotted with rust. The structure looked improvised. It stood under the shade of a large tree with STOP and HALT painted in red letters on its trunk. The officers rose to their feet to address the soldier who had been questioning us. The three of them huddled, cradling their assault rifles as they deliberated.

Our driver cracked his knuckles.

"There is no time for this," my father muttered.

The trip was taking longer than it should. We had lost time at two earlier checkpoints. We had stopped once for my carsick eight-year-old cousin, Joyce, to vomit on the side of the road, twice for my great-uncle Selassie and Great-Aunt Wilhemina to use the bathroom, and had lost more than half an hour while my Uncle Innocent bought kelewele and caramel-vanilla soda for everyone in the van.

Despite having been unemployed for more than two years, Uncle Innocent had been very charitable in the weeks since my grandmother's death. Whether this new openhandedness had any correlation to the bank wire transfers from my father for funeral expenses had yet to be revealed.

My father lowered his head. Facedown on the backs of his hands, resting on the top of the seat in front of him, I thought of my father considering the meaning of his life and the things he might have done differently. He had wanted to carry his mother in a hearse, something white and elegant, but to get her home he needed a vehicle that could navigate the unpaved roads off the motorway. When he helped strap her coffin onto the back of a flatbed he nearly cried from shame. He had been quiet for most of the ride. I imagined him thinking about her body in the truck trailing behind us, rocking in her wooden box to the bumps in the asphalt, head shaking slowly like whenever she disapproved of something, like when he was little, and he and the city boys of Adabraka would jump street gutters and throw stones at each other for fun. His mother would scold them for trying to ruin their school uniforms, sucking her teeth and shaking her head, the small wattle beneath her chin trembling. She was so soft, shea butter smooth. At the morgue her skin was scaly, stiff, and frozen. They had to keep her cold enough for my father and me to fly in for the burial. Looking at her then, it must not have seemed natural to him how death can change a person forever. When my father wept into the receiver in the early hours of Eastern Standard Time, his brother, Uncle Innocent, repeating solemnly, "Maama's dead. Maama's dead," history began to change around them. My grandmother, a fierce authoritarian, now became a compassionate caregiver. She was known to slap her children or rap them on the head without provocation. In her passing, all her seemingly random acts of violence were validated. *God rest her soul*, she had done all she could with what she had been given. *God rest her soul*, she had tried her best to give them the lessons they desperately needed. "Do you know why infants cry when they are born?" she would ask them, never expecting an answer. "Because at birth the spirits pinch our children in order to introduce them to pain. Never forget that to live is to suffer." My father never forgot. At an early age he decided that if his life in Africa was to be nothing but hurt, then he would have to get a new one in a new world without spirits.

He resolved to immigrate to America if only to ensure that any children he ever hoped to have would not also be fated to sadness. He meant to be a better father than his own, about whom he couldn't remember much more than accessories: a beard, a pipe, a pair of glasses, and a cane. His father died young—young it seemed to him now that he was nearing sixty. *He was a good man*, they all said, years later, after the coup. *He served alongside President Nkrumah in the first Ghanaian government*, his obituary read. The truth was far less impressive. He was a mid-level bureaucrat at the Ministry of Food and Agriculture—a passive, quiet, easily forgettable man who only met Nkrumah once in passing while shopping at the Makola Market. My grandfather cast no shadow, leaving no indelible marks on his family besides the effects of his absence.

Auntie Delores, my father's sister and the eldest of the three children, had been the closest to my grandfather before he passed. A year after his death, she cut her hair short and started smoking and talking back. In an ultimate act of rebellion, Auntie Delores married a white man, Aric, from Rotterdam.

"Fifteen minutes past noon," Uncle Aric announced from the front passenger seat, tapping the face of his Swiss wristwatch. "We have a chance to recover the time lost if these men hurry."

Auntie Delores met Uncle Aric while she was at university. She was a first-year and he was visiting distinguished faculty. She ran away with him to the Netherlands when she was nineteen. Auntie Delores never spoke to my grandmother again, but she continued to write letters to the family, usually to gloat about how much better life was overseas. The funeral was the first time she had returned to Ghana.

"I once wrote a piece about this for a journal in London," Uncle Aric continued. "I addressed global misinterpretations of Sub-Saharan Africa and stereotypes reinforced by military men brandishing machine guns."

My father wanted to tell Uncle Aric to shut up. He didn't like the overt references to his own success or the way he turned everything into a platform to explain what was wrong with Africa. In one of her letters, my father remembers Auntie Delores affirming Uncle Aric as "the most revered professor of African studies." She once called him a "prominent authority of the continent."

Auntie Delores cleared her throat. She was seated on the second row, behind the console between Uncle Aric and the driver. She spoke loudly enough for everyone in the van to hear. "Aric, this isn't a faculty mixer. Most of the people in this van won't know the journal you're planning to boast, and I am sure they are even less familiar with your work."

My father laughed and then sat up quickly, wincing. He had been having trouble with his lower back, sharp flashing pains at the base of his spine. He often had to park his cab and walk around. It wasn't good for him sitting this long. He pulled his arm behind him and tried to knead his lumbar with the heel of his palm. He twisted, maneuvering around Uncle Innocent's elbow, trying to get a better reach. Over his shoulder he caught me staring at a sunbeam bouncing off the face of Uncle Aric's watch.

My father never felt more accomplished than on the day I was born. He toasted with friends to an American son with Ghana in his veins. He envisioned raising a better version of himself. Unfortunately, parenting proved to be a series of disappointments. I displayed neither talent for sports nor an early interest in women. When his infidelity led to divorce, he seemed grateful to have an excuse not to see me.

But my father had confronted his own mortality in the shadow of my grandmother's death, and perhaps, fearing no one might be obligated to bury him, he began to regret having let so much time pass. I was old now, sixteen, maybe too old, but I'm certain he heard me scribbling into my journal behind him and hoped it might provide a means for some type of reconciliation.

He smiled at me through gritted teeth. "You okay?" he asked.

I looked down into my notebook. "Yes. I'm fine."

"Good," he said. "You're writing."

"Yes."

"About Ghana?"

"Maybe."

"Good...Good."

Next to me, by the window, Cousin Junior was eating the last of the kelewele. He was much older than my father and with the exception of his cheeks, fat and puffy with food, his face was filled with creases. Cousin Junior bent over to pick up some discarded funeral programs from the floor of the van. He tucked them into the greasy butcher paper that had carried the seasoned crisps of fried plantain and turned it into a ball with his hands.

As he slid open a window to throw out the sphere of crinkled paper, my father asked him what he was doing. Cousin Junior's fist froze outside the van, the paper gripped tightly between his dry, cracked fingers.

"You can't do that," my father said.

Uncle Innocent shook his head. He said, "Brother, this is Africa."

"What does that mean, this is Africa?" Uncle Aric asked.

Uncle Innocent smiled. "It means this isn't America or Europe. Cousin Junior is from the bush, not the city. No one told him he could not throw a little trash on the ground."

"That is the problem," Uncle Aric said. "That is exactly the attitude, and the language, they use to diffuse accountability."

"And who are they?" asked Auntie Delores.

"Anyone that cites the Europeans and colonization as the root of all of Africa's current problems."

"Wait. They aren't? It isn't?"

"I am serious, Delores. I hear that expression often. 'This is Africa.' It is very dangerous. It suggests that Africa is irreparable." Uncle Aric went on. "Where is the government in all this? Why hasn't Cousin Junior been taught to recycle?"

My father listened.

Uncle Innocent sucked his teeth and rubbed his forehead. "So much talk," he said.

The driver shushed the van.

The soldier was returning.

Cousin Junior pulled the ball of trash inside.

"Apologies," the soldier said. "It is procedure." He tapped the license on the side-view mirror before returning it to the driver. "Did this vehicle receive proper inspection before being registered with the DVLA?"

"Yes, sir," the driver replied.

"Good," the soldier said.

The soldier looked up the road and then back the way we had come. Although the sun beat down on his wool beret and heavy army fatigues, he did not perspire. He stepped away from the van and waved at the truck carrying my grandmother. He motioned for the other driver to go around. The white pickup pulled slowly into the opposite lane and rolled ahead of our van. The vehicle paused in front of us, hesitant. The two officers who had been waiting under the makeshift shelter jogged onto the motorway. They shouted. One moved to the passenger side of the truck and the other went around to the driver. They tapped the barrels of their rifles on the windows.

The truck jumped forward.

It became a fuzzy white dot on the horizon and then vanished.

My father shifted in his seat.

"The men in that truck were following you?" the soldier asked.

"Yes," said the driver shakily.

"They don't know how to get there?" asked the soldier.

"No."

The soldier smiled again. He reached inside the van and dropped a hand on the driver's shoulder. "Ah, we understand. We are family men. Don't worry. We want you to catch up with them. All we ask for is cooperation and some support." He removed his hand and whistled to the other officers. They joined him by the driver's window.

"We need to see some identification from everyone in the vehicle," the soldier said.

Uncle Innocent slid his window open.

My father shook his head.

Uncle Innocent addressed the soldier calmly and with a sense of familiarity. "Friend, I assure you we're not the type of people you're looking for. We're good people. Everyone in this vehicle is a law-fearing citizen or a documented visitor."

Even though they were only separated by fifteen months, my

father was very different from Uncle Innocent. Uncle Innocent had the disposition of a charismatic priest. He liked to say, "All is best for God's divine will." He always smiled, even during the funeral, even while reprimanding family members who openly grieved. "Why are you crying? Was Maama not a good Christian woman? Do we not have faith in the Lord and Savior Jesus Christ, through whom all things are possible? Then we accept that she is with God and should not be so foolish as to mourn." Like many things that threatened to crush Uncle Innocent, the loss of my grandmother broke over the rock that was his absolute faith.

"Of course," the soldier replied. "I only need to see some of that documentation."

"This is ridiculous," said Uncle Aric, crossing his arms tightly over his chest. Uncle Aric's ears were turning red. He opened his mouth to speak but paused when he seemed to notice the soft murmurs behind him. Next to me, Auntie Edna, a longtime friend of the family, was whispering to her husband, Uncle Dexter. Their eyes were locked on the white man likely to cause trouble.

"I am sorry." Uncle Aric leaned across the driver. "We have been in this van all day. It is very hot, and the air conditioning barely works. All we want to do is put my family's mother to rest.

If we have given you any reason to suspect us of anything, please, just tell us."

The soldier leaned into the window. His eyes traced over us, from the back row forward, an invisible S from Cousin Junior to me to Auntie Edna to Uncle Dexter to my father's first cousins, the twins, Kofi and Kwame, to my father to Uncle Innocent to Great-Aunt Wilhelmina to Joyce to Auntie Delores to Great-Uncle Selassie. The soldier's gaze hovered over the driver before returning to Uncle Aric.

"Many Nigerians have tried to enter Ghana recently," the soldier said. "They are trying to escape political and economic unrest. No oil subsidies. No food. Gangs. Protests and violence. Muslims in the north fighting with Christians in the south. Days ago, I heard of a group of Muslims opening fire at a beer parlor, and then later I heard Christians retaliated by setting fire to an Islamic school full of children. Ah, no good at all. They are saying there will be another civil war."

"You think some of us are illegal immigrants from Nigeria?" Uncle Aric asked.

The soldier pointed to Uncle Innocent. "He confessed that some in the vehicle are not from Ghana."

"That was not a confession," said Uncle Aric.

The soldier eyed the driver. "Do you have identification to prove you are a citizen of this country?"

"Our driver showed you his license," said Uncle Aric.

"It could be a fake."

"Sir, surely you do not expect people to carry their birth certificates."

The officers shuffled closer to the van.

"My white brother, let us not over-flog the issue. My men and I, we are humble fighters. We protect people. Don't make us feel unwanted. If we are disillusioned, if we are discouraged, we may fold our arms and sit down, and then there could be serious consequences. The road is not safe. My friends and I, all we are asking for is some support. For our service."

"Aric, this does not have to be complicated," Uncle Innocent said.

Uncle Aric turned to the back of the van. "I do not think you fully understand what this man is insinuating."

"I think I do," said Uncle Innocent. "I think I have known all my life, better than you."

Uncle Innocent asked the soldier if there was a fee we could pay for not having the necessary information. "A toll perhaps?"

The soldier released his rifle and let it hang from its strap across his shoulder. "For our service some have made donations. For some small thing to eat, eh?" He made a bowl with his hands. He laughed. "Empty. See?"

"What if we choose not to make a donation?" Uncle Aric asked.

The van shook gently to my father's bouncing leg. Relatives who were not as fluent in English squirmed in their seats. Kofi and Kwame whispered to each other in Ewe.

"That's no good," the soldier replied.

He ordered the driver to exit the vehicle.

Without the hum of the engine, every movement was louder: the rattle of the keys as they were pulled from the ignition, the squeaks of dry palms on polished guns, the groan and creak of the van door as the driver stepped out, the soft clicks from the officer's boots. There was the sound of the scuffle and then the hard thump of a skull slammed against the road.

"Stop this immediately," Uncle Aric screamed.

"It is procedure," said the soldier.

The officers hooked arms with the driver and hoisted him up from the asphalt. He hung between them. His head slumped. Strings of blood stretched past his swollen lips.

"I have friends at news organizations that can turn something like this into a story," Uncle Aric cried. "Government officials asking for bribes, detaining and beating innocent people..."

The soldier slammed the driver's side door and leaned in through its open window. He pointed his finger and turned it into a fist. His knuckles hovered a foot from Uncle Aric's face.

He didn't raise his voice.

"You have openly accused me of bribery. You bring shame to my men and me. I do not want your money."

The officers dragged the driver around the front of the van and off the road.

"What do you want?" Uncle Aric asked.

The soldier folded his arms. After a long silence he smiled again, the same friendly grin he had given when he first approached the van.

"That is a very beautiful watch," he said. "Could you give me the time?"

My father's shoulders rose and fell with his quickening breaths. A new ring of sweat had formed around the collar of his dress shirt. I imagined my father thinking of his mother, speeding away in the back of a truck without a clear destination. Getting my grandmother to Atiavi, making sure she made it home, was just as much about putting his own soul to rest. Completing her journey to eternal peace had appeared to be his last chance for contrition, a means of absolving himself from the guilt of leaving.

My father glanced at me over his shoulder. He could no longer hear me writing. My cheap pen was still. But I was paying attention, saving the story.

My grandfather had been a storyteller too. He often told his children about the one and only time he had dealt with a snake. As a young boy he would paddle a small wooden fishing boat across the lagoon, from Keta to Atiavi, to visit the girl who would become my grandmother. One day, while dragging the boat to the water, he saw a snake coiled on the bank. He stayed clear of the serpent, fearing it might bite, but when the nose of the boat touched the water the snake called over to him. My grandfather tried to ignore the serpent, but it slithered closer when he stepped into the hull. The snake explained that it had been separated from its family on the other side of the river. The distance was too far to swim. The snake asked to be ferried across. My grandfather felt sorry for the snake. As my grandfather had often been instructed to do as Christ would do, he agreed, picking up the serpent and placing it into the boat. The snake shared jokes as my grandfather paddled and they laughed together. Once they reached the other side, my grandfather leapt out and pulled the boat onto the shore. He removed the snake, setting it gently on the sand. The snake thanked him and as my grandfather turned to walk away the serpent bit his heel. My grandfather fell to the ground, screaming in pain. The venom felt like hot porridge in his veins. He cried out, shouting at the creature as it reared its head up to strike again. He asked the serpent why it was attacking him. "Because I am a snake," it said.

This is how my grandfather lost most of the feeling in his left foot, which is why he used a cane until the day he died. My father didn't believe in talking snakes. He was certain the story was only a retelling of an old folktale, but the moral had always felt true to him. Things are fixed in their nature. My father had carried this lesson most of his life. When he was young he saw his home only as a place of ancestry, an old earth squared tightly in the past. Ghana was always developing but never came any closer to being First World. Most of his family and friends dreamed of leaving, but even those who resolved to stay and make a life for themselves chose to accept the country as they had always known it to be. The people my father knew dismissed the extreme poverty, the underfunded schools, and the lack of public services. The people he knew acknowledged but did little to confront corruption. All over Ghana, there were men and women aware of the political realities and ready to exploit them: citizens, officials, lawmakers, bureaucrats, and army lieutenants with aspirations never to be realized, forgotten on country roads.

"You are joking?" Uncle Aric said.

The soldier looked to my cousin Joyce.

"Do not worry, sweetheart," the soldier said. "The adults have almost finished talking."

Through the large window on the sliding passenger door, my father watched the officers disappear with the driver behind the single tin wall of their shelter.

Auntie Delores leaned forward to squeeze her husband's hand.

"This timepiece is guaranteed accurate within one minute per year. It was an anniversary present from my wife."

My father continued to stare beyond the tinted glass, looking over the countryside. We had seen similar terrain speed past us that day, fields of tall thin grass, short trees, and shrubs, sprouting from the red-clay earth, running on for miles into distant lines of thick forest. Villages would materialize from the flatland, shallow towns built around the two-lane highway, the only paved road, shanty churches and sun-bleached cement houses all one faded pastel pink, their bottoms freckled with mud. When the van slowed for goats, chickens, and hogs, vendors sprang from their three-walled shops. Women with large baskets of bagged water balanced on their heads, children dragging machetes and sacks of coconuts, slapping the roof or beating on the side in hopes that we might stop and buy. My father must have noticed, peering past the sellers, that even in these distant pockets of the country there now stood mobile phone kiosks, Internet cafés, and payday loan shops.

"Soon there won't be much difference between here and there," my father had said to me when we boarded the plane at Dulles International. "Perhaps there never was much difference."

"Then why'd you leave?" I said. I didn't wait for his reply

before pulling headphones over my ears. I pretend to listen to music on my MP3 player. I tried my best not to show how desperately I wanted an answer.

Was it foolish of my father, driving a cab all day, every day, day in, day out, wrecking his spine on potholes and speed bumps just to go deeper into debt? For nineteen years he had struggled in the States to own, truly own, little more than the clothes on his back. Life in Ghana could be hard, but America was difficult in its own way. Is it possible that we could flee to better worlds, adopt a new country, a new language, a new name, and never escape the circumstances of our birth? If our lives are fated to sadness, doesn't that mean we can suffer anywhere?

"No," my father said. "Aric, do not give him anything."

My father began to yell at the soldier. It was something about the past, and maybe the future. I had trouble following his rant as he moved further from English into Ga and then a mixture of Ewe and Twi, and then something I had never heard before, something older, a language that sounded like the song of the earth. But he punctuated it with the word No, punching the ceiling of the van every time he said it. No. No. No. Like cannon fire. Fast and loud, louder than I had ever heard him. I raised my hands to cover my ears. The officers reappeared from behind the tin wall, their guns pointed and ready. My father dug his fingernails into the seat in front of him, rolling onto his feet as if he might try to crawl over Auntie Delores. The soldier reached for his assault weapon. One of the officers ran to the van and slid open the passenger cabin door.

My father stopped shouting, his chest heaving, bent at the waist, the top of his back pressed hard to the interior roof.

"Not anymore," he said finally.

Nothing moved in the sudden silence.

Everything was quiet.

My father must have remembered how my grandfather's eyes drooped with sadness in the years leading to his death. Many of my grandfather's colleagues had spoken out against General Kotoka and the soldiers of the National Liberation Council during the 1966 coup. Some of his co-workers had even been arrested in the years that followed during subsequent military occupations. But my grandfather worked hard and kept quiet. He advanced and retired with a pension, and then the weight of all the things he had left unsaid crushed him long before he was dead.

When my father died and the time came for me to plan his eulogy, I knew I wanted to speak of his courage. My wife and I watched the sunset over Accra from the balcony of our apartment. The last bit of daylight sank into the fluorescent orange glow of the city, and I asked her what she thought I should say at the funeral. She was silent for a while. We could hear the baby stirring on the monitor in my hands. "Tell a story. The one with the soldier and the driver," she said. She kissed me before heading inside. I lit a mosquito coil and watched it smolder in the dark. I sat there wondering if my father might be easier to understand in the context of a narrative, or easier to forgive.

The following morning my father's body was flown in from America. I had made the arrangements for his repatriation. Before his passing he had requested that there be no service. "No churches. I just want to go home," he had said. Uncle Innocent, Uncle Aric, and Auntie Delores met me and my family at Kotoka International Airport to receive my father's remains. We drove to Atiavi. At the burial I remembered aloud the fear I saw in the eyes of the officers, their fingers trembling over triggers as they considered this wild man and what they might have to do to quiet him. I talked about the soldier and how he ordered us to leave. "Collect your driver and go," he said, perhaps deciding that killing or arresting us was not worth the attention brought to him and his men.

I continued to share the details committed to my memory, how my father stared defiantly at the military men, how he pushed past Kofi and Kwame to exit the van. I explained how he walked toward the four-post shelter and how he disappeared behind the structure. A moment later the driver appeared from beyond the tin wall. He was bruised and beaten, his shirt torn and stained with dirt. He hobbled as quickly as he could to the van, holding a hand to his mouth to stop the bleeding. My father followed, walking slowly but purposefully. His back was straight, unburdened. The soldier placed the keys on the hood, and he and his officers retreated to the shade of their shelter.

Standing over my father's grave, I described the welcome breeze through the open windows as we sped away. We rode on in silence, nothing but the sound of air rushing past.

As I told the story, I grew closer to my father than I had ever been while he was alive. I was there again, in the van, but with him, sniffing the air wafting around him, the syrupy aroma of caramel-vanilla soda and fried plantain, and beneath that, the wind brushing over the locks of Auntie Delores' hair, redolent of milk and lavender, like my grandmother. The scent of a ghost.

We would catch the truck carrying my grandmother. They would be waiting for us, parked by a shipping container that had been converted into a small roadside market. We'd stop to buy some mineral water and use the bathroom, and then we would finish our journey to Atiavi. And with every mile put behind us, the land would look a little different.

MEMORIALS

I.

The morning Ernesto died and a glittering cloud of debris and ash swallowed the neighborhood, Beth Gopin was on her way to see him. Beth had called Ernesto and asked him to meet her at Taj Tribeca.

Beth will one day tell me how she first met Ernesto at Taj Tribeca. She was on a blind date with someone else, a junior vice president at a fiduciary management company. When the conversation had begun to include words like *portfolio management, estates, big account,* and *mutual funds*, she excused herself from the table and said she needed to use the bathroom. As she snuck toward an exit to abandon her suitor, Ernesto approached her. Beth remembers accepting his card. He had asked her to call him if things didn't work out with the guy she had come with. He thanked her and then quickly sped out of the restaurant.

Beth will tell me she waited weeks before she called him. She'll say she called because of curiosity, not attraction.

"Admit it," Ernesto had said on their first date. "It was pretty cool the way I asked you out, right? Totally smooth and in control."

And Beth had laughed. Correcting him, she said, "You're joking! You strolled up to me like a shy little boy. The whole time you tapped your foot like a nervous freak."

While Ernesto's arrogance often annoyed Beth, she will later admit to me that she also found his fake confidence endearing. Beth Gopin assures me she never once regretted having kept Ernesto's business card.

Four years after they first met, Ernesto leaned over a plate of chicken chettinad at Taj Tribeca and proposed to her. Beth didn't have to think long before saying yes. Beth will tell me that with Ernesto she could imagine braving the commitments that terrified her: buying a house, having kids, and all the permanence suggested by matrimony.

The day Ernesto died, Beth was on her way to tell him that, after a year of trying, they were finally going to be parents—news Beth felt deserved a celebratory minty Cornish hen hariyali.

Having been propelled from their apartment by the promise of the little pink positive sign, Beth sped to the restaurant and arrived too early for lunch. She decided to wait down the block at the New Amsterdam Library. Beth has spent a thousand hours shelf-reading its stacks, working part-time as a page while going to school. Between answering questions, hunting down books for patrons, and sleeping off hangovers curled beneath study carrels, she developed an affinity for libraries. She discovered gratification whenever she'd find an item that had been misshelved, or when someone complimented her book displays. When she graduated from college, confronted with the prospects of teaching or using her BA in English to write for a living, she chose to return to school for a master's degree in library science. If she didn't have the talent to scribe a great American novel or the patience to show someone else how, at least she could help provide authors and educators with the resources needed to do their jobs better.

Beth pushed through the large, heavy glass doors. She waved at the front desk, although no one who worked there would have been there long enough to know her. Beth climbed the steps to the second floor with care. She walked over to the fiction section and chose a row randomly. Sauntering down the aisle, she extended her arms like a bird about to take flight. She let the tips of her fingers drag along the spines of books, smiling at the thought of never having the time to read them all, especially after the baby arrived. At the end of the shelves, she pulled down a title. Beth will tell me she can't remember the name or its cover, but she recalls for me retreating with the book to a vacant ottoman by a window and thumbing through it casually as she envisioned the new life inside her. Beth first conjured the image of a little girl as gregarious as Ernesto and then a little boy as reserved as herself. Beth would have to have a talk with Ernesto about parenting strategies, education, and faith. Beth did not practice, but Ernesto greatly valued religion, and Beth knew he would want his child to believe in something.

There was a rumble like doom, louder than thunder.

The city paused as Beth looked up from her page.

She'd grown accustomed to the sound of collisions in the city, but this was different, unfamiliar.

Beth tried to dismiss it initially and returned to the book laid open on her lap. She hadn't read a single word. She tried to focus, but soon her thoughts led back to her belly. Staring blankly at the page, she chuckled nervously at the idea of having to rest her books on top of a rounded paunch.

Somewhere in the building phones began to ring. Murmurs grew louder, and Beth could feel the floor tremble as people moved hastily around her, marching up to nearby windows. Her heart skipped; it sank lower in her chest and rested on her stomach. She stood to go downstairs.

Beth joined a wave of others rushing to the main floor and out onto the street.

She'd tell me the day was bright, clear except for a single thick cloud ripping through the sky. Everyone gazed upward at the dark cumulus, a column of smoke creeping toward City Hall. Beth could hear screams coming from windows above her. The air tasted like gasoline.

Crowds gathered on the street, talking fast and pointing. Buildings hemorrhaged people; they poured from offices and apartments. Beth watched large groups move west past Taj Tribeca. She followed.

Beth had walked that block more times than she could remember, never giving much thought to what the street might mean to her. That day, the street was covered in landmarks: the bar where she and Ernesto had toasted when she had accepted her reference librarian position, the lamp post where they had hailed their first taxi together back to his place, the spot under the awning where they had once tried to wait out the rain and where Beth had first realized that she loved him.

She remembers that night vividly.

Beth remembers Ernesto saying, "You know Beth can mean 'house' in Hebrew."

"Are you calling me fat?"

He stuttered, trying to clarify, before seguing into an explanation of how much he cared for her. He explained how she made him feel always at home. And even though she had heard other couples say similar words, the sentiment felt new and exciting to her.

"It's okay," she said. "Me too."

Beth continued following the mass of pedestrians to an intersection, and when she looked up she saw smoke billowing from a skyscraper. Tiny figures, thrashing like bodies, rained from the building. Beth closed her eyes and counted to five, like Ernesto often did whenever he became anxious or angry.

Achat.

Shtayim.

Shalosh.

Arba.

Chamesh.

Ernesto liked to list the many words for faith—aman, mahseh, mibtah—whenever things went wrong. Beth had always admired his conviction. Ernesto stayed faithful, even when believing was difficult.

A hundred taxis began honking their horns all at once.

Beth opened her eyes to see an airliner diving toward Ernesto's office.

In that moment, all she could think to do was pray.

I'm sitting at my desk in third period, a social science class called Problems of the Twentieth Century. The lights are off, and our teacher, Mr. Schwartz, is about to show a documentary about the bankruptcy of a city in Michigan following the collapse of its chief industry. Mr. Schwartz stands beside the television and VCR at the front of the room, ranting about wage gaps and huge disparities in wealth and how everything is connected.

I'm not paying too much attention to his tirade. I am writing a note to pass to Beth Habash in the hall between classes. This semester, our schedules have us heading in opposite directions. We've stayed in contact through our letters. They never really say anything, but it is nice having someone to write to. This particular note has swelled to two pages, front and back, explaining in detail all the tortures I'd rather endure than listen to Mr. Schwartz pontificate about the correlation between floundering economies and deteriorating race relations.

I don't really think much about stuff like that, unlike Beth. She cares about everything. She says being half Palestinian makes her more sensitive to the suffering of others. She once told me, "Churches are people, gospels in motion, walking cathedrals."

Beth's deep. She only smiles when she's with me.

I'm trying a lot harder this year, trying to make up for nearly getting held back two years ago, hoping that maybe Beth and I can go to college together next fall.

Mr. Schwartz turns around to push the tape into the VCR, and my seventh-period history teacher, Mr. Torrez, charges into the classroom from across the hall. He tells Mr. Schwartz that someone has flown an airplane into a building.

The class stirs nervously as Mr. Schwartz punches the TV Menu button and two shiny metal towers fade into focus, thick smoke rolling out past the gleam of broken windowpanes. I lean closer in my desk, squinting at the flicker of flames behind the dark fog. I'm close enough to hear Mr. Schwartz say, "Bob, I don't think this is an accident."

In the halls after class ends, everyone speaks without commas or periods. The endless streams of speech review what we've all seen: A second commercial airliner slammed into another tower. Several thousand pounds of steel vanished into a wall of glass. I try to avoid joining the murmurs. I follow my usual route because that's what I think Beth would do. She's reliable. She will go the same way she always does. She will know that panicking, congesting the halls like the kids bouncing from one locker to the next, will not help anyone.

Rumors float past my ears that can't be true.

"There are more planes," someone says.

"The nation is under attack," says someone else.

I try to think of other things—my college applications, personal statements, reference letters—but this leads to thoughts of Beth.

I should have seen Beth in the hall by now.

Perhaps she decided to go straight to her AP English class.

Maybe this isn't the quickest route.

Maybe she has tried to evade the crowds on the first floor, going up and over and taking the E-Hall stairway down.

I turn around and speed to her classroom.

I'll be late, but I need to talk to her.

The bell rings when I reach Beth's class. I peer inside through a narrow window in the door. The teacher and students are all fixated on the classroom television.

Some are crying. I can't see the screen. I scan the room. I don't find Beth.

I wait outside the door, but she never shows up.

When I finally arrive to the boys' locker room for gym class, I'm surprised that no one has changed into their workout clothes. All the boys have huddled into Coach Reynolds' office to glare at the thirteen-inch TV sitting on his desk. I have to push through to see.

On the screen there's a fuming crater in the side of another building. Beneath the heads of the muted newscasters, closed captions confirm a third plane crash.

Back in the halls between periods, horseshoes form around rich kids lending out their cellular phones for people to call family. Wealthy bullies, usually starved for catastrophe, have found the best in themselves dispatching messages and reporting on the disaster.

I overhear Margaret Bowen, one of Beth's middle-school tormentors. Margaret says there's been a fourth plane crash in a field. Yesterday, Margaret was a liar inventing the kind of gossip that put other girls' names on bathroom stalls. Today, she is as reputable and up to date as the news ticker scrolling across the bottom of classroom TV screens.

Tomorrow is hard to imagine.

But the class bells keep things moving forward, reminding me that there still might be time and order. The chimes are faithful constants, and each ring promises a next, a day when this is past.

I shuffle into my next period. There are kids everywhere, lining the walls, gathered at the front, sitting cross-legged around Ms. Thackston's desk. Some teachers have abandoned their classes, forcing neighboring teachers to house stray students. Standing at the back near my desk is a girl who has third period with Beth. Her name is Alicia. I move to my seat as Ms. Thackston asks everyone to be considerate of others. I offer my desk to Alicia. Her eyelids are puffy and red from crying. She shakes her head solemnly, declining. Ms. Thackston moves to the corner of the room, stepping over the kids sprawled on the floor, and sits on the edge of her desk. She grabs a remote from a stack of student essays and raises the volume of the TV.

I whisper to Alicia under the blaring headline news. I ask her if she's seen Beth.

She says yes, this morning before school, but Beth never came to class.

I nod and then turn to stare past the students leaned against the window.

I'm on the third floor, so now I can see the military helicopters, news choppers, and fighter jets tearing across the sky.

Beth says everything is temporary.

I reach into my pocket and pull out the note I had written earlier. It's folded like a paper football. The triangle shape makes it easier to slide into Beth's palm as we pass. I poke the tips of my fingers with its pointed edges.

There is a collective gasp, and then the horrorstruck pops of hands over gaping mouths. I look to the wall-mounted television at the corner of the room. Massive buildings collapse into plumes of tar-colored smoke, cameras switch angles, and then I see my fear mirrored in the eyes of a woman greyed by the dust of the wreckage.

It is the other Beth, Beth Gopin, but I don't know that yet, not until I see the same pained green eyes more than ten years later in a book of grieving faces accompanying a memorial DVD. I won't know for sure until I am standing in Beth Gopin's office at the college library where she works. I will thank her for agreeing to an interview with me for my newspaper article commemorating the anniversary of the atrocities that ended Ernesto's life. She will purse her lips into an anxious smirk, sigh deeply, and then tell me about the day her husband died.

We'll schedule a date for me to take a picture of her with her son. Beth will suggest the day of her son's bar mitzvah. On the steps outside of the temple, after I've taken the photo, she'll ask me where I was when her son's father perished. And although she has heard hundreds of accounts from people attempting to share in her loss, Beth Gopin will listen kindly as I explain how my greatest concern that morning was for a girl who shares her first name, who was safe in bed, sent home from school early with an inner-ear infection. A girl whose love, although transformative, was not strong enough to endure an out-of-state internship, or graduate schools across the country, or a research scholarship in Indonesia, or a long-distance relationship with no visible conclusion.

When I talk with Beth Gopin, I will jump back into myself, return to now, sitting in a classroom desk, watching a police officer drag her away from the rubble.

Now, Beth claws at the cop's forearm, her screams silenced

beneath the broadcaster's commentary. The officer begins to cough violently, choking on the heavy ash. He drops to his knees, and as his hands shoot up around his throat, Beth Gopin runs back toward the fallen structures.

Tears streak her clay face.

Her lips and teeth form a word that looks like *Ernesto*.

The camera doesn't follow her.

Beth is lost in the fallout enveloping the city.

I can see myself leaping from my desk, rushing past Ms. Thackston who calls after me. I'm racing through the halls, my feet squeaking against linoleum. I'm zigzagging from door to door, peeking into every classroom for Beth. I almost fall to the ground sliding onto B-Hall, but I regain my balance and jog faster. We've started running, full speed, the other Beth and I, separately, but together. We have to find them. He needs to know he's going to be a father. She needs to read this note. We've made plans with someone, and we shout their name through the halls and streets.

LALITA RATTAPONG'S
NEW MICROWAVE

I'm having trouble with Lalita Rattapong's new microwave, is-sues with distance. Like, can the neighbors feel the universe fold in on itself whenever she reheats leftover panang? Do they hear time collide, past in present, echoes from a world older than the one they thought they knew, screeching in their ears like twisting metal? Can they hear the ding of the micro-wave's tiny bell, snapping Lalita Rattapong back to now, her cup of noodles waiting hot and ready, her bare feet caked with fresh mud from the sixteenth century, the wet earth of an early Portuguese settlement staining the checkerboard tiles of her kitchen floor?

Is this the point of entry, a proper start to a story about a lonely woman and her microwave time machine? And what next? Will Lalita Rattapong share her discovery with Asami and Robert, two of her fellow copyeditors at the *Bangkok Post*? Aren't they both well educated and better traveled? Will she explain to them how the microwave appeared to her in the labyrinths of the Jatujak Market beneath an ALL PURCHASES FINAL sign, how the microwave seemed to her a perfect blend of vintage design, atomic but ornamental style, art deco, with curving sides that plume at the top like an old-timey radio and thin white lines that reminded her of South Beach and spring break and studying in America? Does she tell them how the microwave brings the whole kitchen together, the warmth of its pastel ocean-water blue adding some much needed color against her exposed cinderblock wall without overshadowing the intention of her industrial aesthetic? Does Lalita tell them about the vendor: a small, wrinkled woman with no teeth and only a pinky and a thumb for a right hand? Does she mention how, when asked about the microwave, the vendor seemed not to recognize it? What about the old woman selling the appliance for just 900 baht without haggling? What about while carrying the microwave up three flights of stairs to her condo, Lalita found the words "Made in" embossed on its back panel with no country of manufacturing? Were these early indications?

What do Lalita Rattapong's friends say then? Do they help her speculate on the origins of the microwave? Will Asami point out that it isn't uncommon for manufacturers to unload faulty merchandise on developing countries, and will this prompt Robert to add a joke about how at that very moment some kids in Mexico could be kicking around a dinosaur egg that their mother discovered while warming empanadas?

After they fail to offer Lalita any suggestions for a good repairman, do Asami and Robert move into a dialogue about the apparent death of skilled labor? Does it sound something like this?

Why don't we know anyone who can fix a microwave? Does anyone really use his or her hands anymore?

Do you ever think we might see the end of trade careers?

Who is to say it's not possible? How many kids these days want to grow up to work on appliances?

Will craftsmen have a place in a knowledge-based economy?

Right?

You have a point, but wouldn't some form of craftsmen endure?

Care to give an example?

What about the writers?

Are you suggesting there is a natural comparison between the craftsman and the creative artist?

Wordsmiths?

We aren't talking about metaphorical craftsmen, are we? Aren't writers the only people who generally view what they do as using craft? We're talking about people who actually build things, right? People who toil?

Don't they build worlds? Don't they toil to craft new narratives?

But do they know anything about hard labor?

What about labors of love?

And does this discussion, riddled with the type of sweeping generalizations and pseudo-intellectual pontification common among cynical expatriates and people of a certain socio-economic class, provide Lalita Rattapong an opportunity for reflection? While Asami and Robert debate whether their terminal degrees allow them to better identify with blue-collar workers and trade union activists, will Lalita reconsider her buyer's remorse? Is this conversation indicative of the problem with Lalita Rattapong's life, shallow but giving the appearance of depth, a series of provocative questions that lead to insignificant conclusions like those used on the cover of general interest magazines or to title a dissertation?

Hadn't she wished for something to disrupt the banality of her existence, something to make her life as exciting as the world reporters whose work came across her desk day after day? Is the microwave the conflict or the catalyst? Had she ever felt more connected to the world, more purposeful, than when tiptoeing through random points in history? How far away and unimportant had her problems felt, sneaking around Bangkok during foreign occupation, dodging Japanese soldiers and resistance movements, trying not to reshape the past? When was the last time she worried about having left Greg after six years without serious talk of engagement? Wasn't it true that since discovering the microwave she had given little thought to the fear of sleeping alone forever? Is it because forever didn't seem so long anymore?

Later, when Lalita Rattapong says goodbye to Asami and Robert for the evening and heads home, will she get off at an earlier stop on the skytrain to purchase some frozen calamari rings from a Western-style supermarket? Will she rush to her condo and straight to the kitchen?

Can I skim here, past the seemingly insignificant moments that define a life, Lalita throwing her laptop bag on her Scandinavian modern–style couch, Lalita reaching for a French paring knife, cutting into the packaging, the cold block of squid slapping hard against a plate? Can I leap forward in time until finally she is shutting the small door to the microwave, thinking carefully about the correlation between the timer and the time spent in the past?

What is the longest she's been gone? Twenty minutes? Thirty minutes? Was she defrosting tilapia or popping popcorn? Does the process depend on the item being cooked? Accepting that she has no way of calculating this anomaly, will Lalita Rattapong twist the microwave's chrome dial back to ten? Does she surrender to the now familiar sensation, something like a hand reaching in past her navel, grabbing the base of her spine, and pulling forward as if trying to turn her inside out?

And then where is she? How long does it take her mind to get oriented after being yanked through the space-time continuum, for Lalita's brain to register that she is standing alone, minutes before dawn, in a damp meadow with large trails cutting through the acres of matted grass like number signs? When she looks up at the sky, does it reveal some clue? Can she remember a time when the stars have ever been so close? Does she recognize the smell of elephant shit from trips to the zoo as a child, and watching live reenactments of wars fought on the backs of pachyderms? Is this the site of a battle she studied in grade school, Yuddhahatthi or the Battle of Nong Sarai?

Are those dark mounds people, peeking out from the tall, thin leaves?

When the wind turns will she smell blood?

When Lalita considers the hundreds of soldiers who must have trampled through the clearing, soldiers who might still be in the area, ready to rape and kill her, does she decide to head to the forest and wait in the trees until she is returned to the future? Are her flat-soled canvas shoes soaked through to her feet? When she takes her first steps, do they make a loud squishing sound, arousing the attention of a wounded man just a few yards away? When he starts to call out—his Thai is old, formal—does Lalita drop to the ground, startled? How long will she stay crouched down, one knee pressed into the soft soil, cursing to herself, debating her options? Should she make a run for the forest or wait where she is in hopes of going undiscovered? How long will Lalita stay hidden, swatting mosquitoes away from her face, listening to the man groan in pain? How many times does he plead for death before she decides to abandon her rule about never getting involved, rise to both feet, and walk toward the sound of his voice?

Standing over him, his body outlined by the grass, does his dark skin fade into the shadows? In the silence that follows, does Lalita imagine how strange she must look to him, her jeans and blouse, her short bobbed hair haloed by the fading moon? Can she hear, in his silence, his disappointment in being discovered by a woman?

When he asks *What are you?*, does she reply *A traveler*?

Is that enough for him?

Does the wounded warrior grunt knowingly?

Does Lalita notice his breath quicken and then become shallow? Can she hear him dying over the sound of her own heart beating in her ears? Does she agree to stay with him, only as long as she can, although he never asked her to?

With the night receding and the sun peeking over the canopy of trees, will Lalita Rattapong see for the first time that the man is a boy not much older than sixteen? Does the boy remind her of her little brother, if she hadn't been an only child, or the son she might have had if her life had been different? Can she assume that he has been trampled by an elephant, his sunken chest sloping down to a crushed pelvis, his ravaged legs and torso bridged by a pulp of skin and bone? Before the kid warrior dies, will he motion for Lalita to bend down? Does he swallow hard and ask *Am I remembered?*

What more can she do but stand there in a meadow littered with pieces of cloth and armor, shattered weapons, broken swords, and splintered spears, the bitter aroma of dried blood like rust hugging her skin as she switches her gaze back and forth between the sunrise and the boy, his body broken, like her relationships, like her microwave? Is there a connection? Is all that is broken in her universe the result of a principle of relevance? Narrative structure? Intelligent design?

Waiting for me to bring her back to her present, aren't we both, Lalita Rattapong and I, left to consider the significance of this event, what it all means, the greater implications? Is everything a matter of fate? Do these questions linger long after she is returned to her kitchen, the novelty of her time-machine microwave fading like the smell of burnt calamari?

PREFACE TO TALES OF RIVER

Because that vastly developed country to the north dammed the water, and because water means life and wealth and fate, we were made to suffer here; south of the rapids, in another nation, we now struggle against the river's tepid current.

Our mothers envisioned the river as a benevolent goddess.

Genuflecting on cold sandy banks, baiting hooks and casting nets, listening for whispered prayers in the calm babble, our mothers would thank the goddess for fish and water, greens and driftwood and clay, and for all things provided by the veins of the deity.

But the resolution of the river wanes, and so do the women. Their faith and limbs, woven like tight-thick rope by reeling in gifts from streams, become soft jelly.

Not long ago, our fathers found work with the arms of the river.

Bent over damp earth, farming fields and rice paddies irrigated by creeks and rills, the branches of the watershed mapped our fathers' movements, rest and rise. The men once saw their destinies reflected in

the marsh. A man could pull a future from the moist soil. But our fathers'
vision recedes with the water. Unable to see the next year's harvests,
weary without purpose, many men lie down in the dry dirt. Beneath
drought-ridden crops, they only see death and do not rise again.

During our first lesson with Charlie Marlowe at the schoolhouse, he explained why he had come from that vastly developed country to the north. At university Charlie decided to specialize in limnology, believing he would have a professional advantage over general ecology majors. He told us we could read his graduate thesis on the conservation and management of the Orinoco and its drainage basin online in JSTOR. He wrote a web address on the chalkboard in case we wanted to find it later at an Internet café. Following graduation, Charlie had discovered many of his skills were not transferable. Unemployed and desperate to avoid living with his parents again, he accepted a position teaching foreign language to adults abroad.

Charlie concluded his introduction by stating his excitement to spend time in a real agrarian society. He said he looked forward to giving back. These last words impelled many of us to question what Charlie thought he had taken and what he planned to return.

Charlie wanted us to talk about ourselves. He asked to know why we were here.

Only Coventina raised her hand to speak.

She didn't wait for Charlie to acknowledge her before addressing him.

Charlie Marlowe's face exposed his surprise at Coventina's fluency, her command of his native tongue, and how her ideas cascaded from her mouth, a succession of clauses dangling over her lips before falling into a continuous thought. Coventina may have misinterpreted Charlie's question, or, having recognized the inherent ambiguity in his query, decided to explore another interpretation. She began by telling Charlie about our mothers and fathers. She started at the beginning:

Because we were born in the shadow of the river and we took our first steps on the shores of its tributaries, or due to that wet divinity shaping us in her image, our bodies are mostly water. Our lives are anchored to the ebb and flow. The surface reflects our image.

We trace our history with river stones.

Each of us carries stories from our parents of the many instances neighboring tribes and countries tried to conquer us. Colonizers could not survive the river's floods. Each group of invaders was defeated by fever and rot.

Coventina told Charlie more than he had expected to hear, but Charlie sat down and listened, because he was in a position to, and because that was all he could do.

We've seen many foreign language teachers, but Charlie Marlowe remains one of the most memorable. He spent a lot of time by himself and didn't go out in the evenings to the bars to sing karaoke with the other foreign instructors. Many of us saw Charlie strolling around town alone. Charlie carried a notebook everywhere, and he'd often stop suddenly to write his observations. He'd open his journal to note the geometry of an abandoned rice silo, or record the smell of the open-air fish market and the number of empty stalls, or mark the shush of his feet over the fine layer of sand that covered all our walkways, roads, and floors.

Charlie also wrote down comments he heard in the classroom. It started during a lesson on producing cover letters and resumes.

Charlie was explaining the importance of finding an occupation that makes one happy.

He said, "Where I'm from, we say, 'If you choose a job you love, you'll never have to work a day in your life.'"

Coventina raised her hand and said, "I'd rather have purpose than happiness."

"Can't you have purpose and be happy?" Charlie asked.

"Purpose is a responsibility to others. Happiness is about you. The work should be about others or it is selfish."

Shaking his head, Charlie smiled the way adults do when children say something beyond their understanding. He asked Coventina for her permission to write what she had said into his journal. Coventina paused to think. She said yes, and then told Charlie he should write down what the rest of us had to say too.

From then on, Charlie regularly stayed after class to copy some of our expressions to paper. One afternoon, as she exited the door to the study room, Coventina stopped to ask Charlie what he intended to do with all the words he had culled. Charlie admitted he wasn't sure, but he felt compelled to compile observations. He said studying rivers had taught him to follow the smallest brook to big revelations.

Charlie Marlowe's note-taking would of course lead to writing *Tales of River*, a collection of interviews, photographs, watershed maps, and poetic prose redefining the limits of the ecological memoir. Fifteen years after its first printing, the wide critical acclaim and commercial success of *Tales of River* continues to bring much needed attention to our community and provide us a platform from which to share our own stories with the globe. Charlie Marlowe held the door open for famed essayists like Alga Benjuan and Geffer Lupope, and even fiction writers like me.

In its first incarnation, *Tales of River* was very different. Marlowe had initially envisioned the book as a noir novel following a foreign language instructor abroad in an unfamiliar rural hamlet. When the instructor is inexplicably tasked with having to solve the disappearance of one of his students, he uncovers a greater conspiracy involving all of the villagers.

Charlie Marlowe revealed the plot to the class and asked for our opinion. Charlie said he had always wanted to write a novel, and his father had a close friend who served as an executive at a big publishing house. Charlie believed he could sell the story. Although most of us enjoyed Charlie's original premise, Coventina—the person to whom Charlie would inevitably dedicate *Tales of River*—did not applaud the concept. And she told him so. In response, Charlie decided to model a major character on Coventina. He gave Coventina's appearance to the missing student and femme fatale central to the initial sketches of the narrative. Coventina's description appears in the final version of *Tales of River* as a caption below a photographed ancient wood-cut illustrating a local legend about river nymphs. The depiction of Coventina is the only passage from the book's early fiction manuscript to survive the shift in genre to creative nonfiction.

"A wild bush of mango-red hair covered the scalp of her head, and her skin, blacker than a cocoa bean, blacker than any-one had ever seen in any of the surrounding towns and villages, held a dark emerald hue the color of the murky bottom of the deepest parts of the river. She always wore a long jade skirt lay-ered with a thousand tiny tiles of ornamental rock. The green stones shimmered like fish scales when they caught the light and made a sound like trickling water whenever she moved or shuffled in her desk."

Despite Charlie's efforts to appease Coventina with a perfect fictional doppelgänger, she did not change her feelings about the book. After he completed his first draft, he read passages to her. Still unimpressed, she suggested he tell another story.

Coventina had quickly established herself as the most prom-inent person in the classroom, and she came every Tuesday and

Thursday afternoon for ten months before she disappeared.

Charlie floundered in her absence. He had begun depending on Coventina to translate for him. Whenever he struggled to explain some particularly difficult conjugation or preposition, Charlie's eyes lingered over Coventina's empty seat.

He'd ask us about Coventina, and we'd shrug. We knew nothing about her life. Despite Coventina's talkativeness and coquetry during lessons, she never shared information about herself. After classes we'd head west, back to town, and Coventina would walk in the opposite direction, east, across the rear yard of the schoolhouse. We'd see her figure dissolve into trees lining the steep slope down to the river.

Sometimes students disappear. A supervisor or fellow instructor must have told Charlie to expect people to vanish. When class members evaporated, Charlie would have reminded himself that learning a global language might have no immediate or apparent benefit to a people drying out in poverty.

In the shadow of Coventina's vanishing, we assume Charlie considered all Coventina had said about the circumstances facing young women her age:

There was a time all our daughters could weave or sew.

Girls stayed awake in the evenings seaming clothes and linens. They wove baskets and knitted bags. They fashioned comforts and gave us what we needed to carry what's important.

During the day, daughters pushed canopied handcarts bringing ripe fruit and jugs of cool mineral water. They carried news and messages from one road to the next. They threaded streets together, bound and tethered us to one another, relaying lines of speech.

But then the wells dried up. The fruit shriveled and soured. The narrowing river thinned our waists. And many of our daughters carried the family's financial burden.

Girls followed the river hundreds of miles south to the large port cities along the gulf. Some found jobs cleaning houses. Others discovered another kind of pushing, providing comfort underneath the heavy bellies of businessmen and travelers from that vastly developed country to the north.

Maybe the thought of Coventina far away on her knees prompted Charlie Marlowe to enter the forest behind the schoolyard. Perhaps between the thick bark and crowded branches he heard a sound like the steady babbling of Coventina's long green skirt and followed it to where the trees end on a precipice over the river. We can imagine Charlie pulling off his tie, folding the arms of his shirt and rolling up his pant legs, crouching, gripping roots to scale the sheer drop down to a group of boulders lined along the water.

At the bottom, sat on a large rock, Charlie would have seen young men creeping along the recessed shore. Coventina had mentioned how our sons used to ferry people and goods on the river's broad canals. Without work to occupy them, boys Charlie's age spend most days drunk on plum wine. They stalk the water's edge and throw stones at nothing.

We wonder if Charlie, watching and listening quietly atop his rock, thought of Coventina and if he began to consider his life in the context of other people's stories. Maybe this is the moment Charlie Marlowe first saw reflections of himself amid the thin bodies cursing the damned river and that vast country in the north.

March 28, 2006

HERS & YOURS

SHE IS A COSMOS

Alma feels him mapping the constellations of her freckles. He's tracing the Little Dipper on her arm with his thumb. She is happy to find that she doesn't feel easy. In fact, there is a burgeoning sense of satisfaction, like she has found something that was really well hidden. She feels sound.

His hand is making circles on her lower back. His eyes are closed again, but he's awake and smiling. Neither of them appears to be in a hurry to leave.

It had started at a bar. Alma can't remember the name of it. She was just looking for a dark, loud place to get lost. The day had been difficult and she wasn't ready to be alone in the house with her mother. Alma sat in a corner, trying to vanish into the wall, sipping a ginger ale, counting and recounting the hours until her train was scheduled to leave the next morning.

She had noticed him watching her for several minutes before he approached. He introduced himself. He didn't offer to buy her a drink. Alma tried to dismiss him, but he was persistent.

He asked her simple questions at first: What's your name? Where do you work? Do you live in town?

Alma. I'm a student. I'm from here. Her eyes scanned the bar for an escape.

He asked more questions and her answers became monosyllabic. Where are you coming from tonight? Where are you headed? When he sensed that he had asked about something sensitive, he followed with something easy and non-threatening. Do you have any hobbies? What type of music do you listen to? When Alma stopped responding, he nodded politely and began telling her about himself.

He told her about his fear of the ocean. He wasn't afraid of water. He assured her he was a fine swimmer. It's the vastness of the sea, its secret depths, how much it touches, and how much it hides.

He said his favorite color was black.

"Black isn't really a color," Alma cut in. "It is the absence of light. Space is black."

They argued this for a while, but eventually he conceded. His new favorite color would be Alma's favorite color: orange.

He told Alma about his mother and how she had died just a few months ago on his birthday. He told Alma about his decision to quit school and become a writer, and how it bothered his father. They had never really understood each other and with his mother gone, they were drifting further apart.

He asked Alma about her parents.

She told him about helping her father that day and how strong he still looked while reaching for the handle on the steel door of the mover's truck. He could never teach her what not to wear or how to apply eyeliner, but he had taught her how to be tough. She described how he pulled upward to his chest and rolled his wrist to hoist the door over his head, and the way every muscle in his back seemed to tighten as he reached in for the first of the unmarked boxes. He had packed fast and without thinking. Alma could have only guessed at the contents: empty photo albums, moldy vinyl records, unwatched DVDs. Her parents had told her about the separation earlier that week over the phone. They had decided not to tell Alma until after she had finished her final exams. She had come home on the first train and had volunteered to help her father move out of the house.

"Sorry," he said. He took a long sip from his beer and seemed to consider what he might say next. He asked if the divorce was something they both wanted.

Her mother had always loved with hesitation. Half-committed. She had tried to be a dutiful wife and mother, but it always felt forced. After a decade of compromises, she had become distant. When Alma was little and mischievous, her mother would pretend to scold Alma's father when he came home in the evenings. Grinning, she would dare him to guess what his daughter had done that day. Gradually, the playful admonishment began to carry resentment. Tell your daughter to clean her room. Your daughter needs money for classes. I don't know, ask your daughter. Alma could hear how much her mother believed herself to be trapped.

He asked how that made her feel.

"Like a black hole," Alma said.

"Some people are unable to give so much," he said.

Alma nodded. She was sure her mother had never wanted children.

"And how is your father doing?"

Alma explained that her father was a quiet man, a worker, far more expressive with his body than with his words. Watching him that day, Alma could see her father carrying the guilt. It was in the way his knees bent and the way they straightened again, calibrating for something heavier than what was in the boxes. It was in the way he had shuffled on the stone stairway to his new apartment. Part of him questioned whether it was his fault for being too selfish to live alone. He'd never say it, but Alma knew.

Alma remembers bringing in the last box. As she set it down on the floor, there was a clanking inside the cardboard like hard glass. Coffee mugs, maybe, or classical Greek statuettes, ceramic Olympians and armless women, a depiction of Andromeda chained to the rocks forever waiting for Perseus. Tiny hollow people made to gather dust on living room shelves. Alma's father liked to give them as birthday and anniversary gifts. He thought they were classy. Her mother hated them but had never mentioned it, and her father had never thought to ask.

As Alma said goodbye, her father dropped a hand on her shoulder and pulled her into a hug. She stood uncomfortably in his tight embrace. Although he couldn't articulate his gratitude or his love, she understood. She lingered there in her father's strong arms. The front door was open. The sun coming through traced their silhouette on the floor.

Alma thinks about how quickly the world spins. She had been watching shadows move over boxes, and now she is in bed with a stranger. She wonders if these are unrelated events. Are her days like stars, moving through space, seemingly independent of each other until someone draws a connection? Is it the same sun from yesterday, squeezing through the venetian blinds, spotlighting a pile of her clothes on the rug in a column of daylight? On the carpet, the silver pepper-spray keychain she carried with her last night is shimmering in one of the cups of her bra. Alma kept the small canister gripped tightly in her fist as they walked the dark city blocks, talking. She surprised herself by inviting him outside so they could hear each other better. They followed the sidewalk in a giant circle, moving slowly, never running out of things to say. Alma spoke freely. She was honest in a way she had only been with people she never planned to see again. When they arrived back at the bar it was closed. They stood outside for another hour, trying to say goodbye. Alma knew she should leave. She still had to get back to what was now her mother's house and finish packing.

Alma went home with him.

The apartment was sparsely furnished and nothing matched. She took a seat on his futon and she read some of his writing, a short story set in the future on a distant planet. The two human colonies are at war with each other, unaware that the native inhabitants are not extinct and are planning a massive attack of their own. Alma didn't usually like science fiction, and she told him that, but she liked the moral dilemmas, the social politics, and the allusion to Old World mythology. She told him it was good. He asked why.

"I like the theme," she said. "There is this sense throughout that there is always something bigger than ourselves."

He seemed pleased with her answer.

"However," Alma added, "you need a new title. *The Native Threat.* That's a bit obvious, isn't it?"

He smiled. "You might be right," he said.

At four in the morning, Alma decided to stay.

She is looking for patterns and proximity. There are still dots that need connecting. She is charting her own stars.

His heart is beating hard and fast against her ear.

Alma rolls onto her elbows.

"What's your name?" she asks.

TAKEAWAY

The glass surface of the round banquet table buzzed. Outside, anti-government demonstrations jammed the streets of Bangkok. Plastic whistle blasts and the call and response of a hundred megaphones echoed through the humid capital. Sounds of contention burrowed upward through levels of concrete. The protests hummed between Nahm's ears.

Nahm sat with Jason's family in a private dining room on the fourth floor of the Iron Wok Chef. The entrance to the secluded dining area featured a tall red archway ornamented by carvings of spiraling dragons. A wall of windows opened out to a small balcony. Behind a short karaoke stage decorated with blinking Christmas lights, panels of full-length mirrors attempted to give a greater sense of space. But the mirrors reflected the opposite wall and a mural of a foggy Lushan mountain range, trapping dinner guests between identical dark summits and stirring Nahm's anxiety.

To calm herself, Nahm narrowed her concentration on

specific parts of the meal. She tried to identify the various flavors in the shark fin soup. She attempted to calculate the cost of each ingredient passing between her lips. Nahm had developed habits like these selling mango and sticky rice with her mother in front of the headquarters for Kaidee Inter Auto Parts Co., Ltd. During those long hours, she would stare down at one of the cracks in the grimy sidewalk and count the number of expensive shoes that passed over, or she'd look up at the tangled thicket of telephone wires running above her head and imagine where each line finished and began.

Every year Jason had pleaded for Nahm to attend his family's Chinese New Year dinner, and every year she declined, saying she didn't want to go anywhere she wasn't welcome. But tonight she had finally conceded.

Jason leaned over to whisper, "This is not as nice a restaurant as the one we had last year."

Nahm nodded.

The rotating tray at the center of the tabletop squeaked, some of the silverware had soap spots, Jason's chair had one shorter leg, and the karaoke machine only played folk songs. Thankfully, the deep-fried soft shell crab claws served with plum sauce were delicious, and Nahm said she liked the lychee fruit salad.

Jason's father enjoyed the glass noodles with baked shrimp and ordered a second plate for the table. Jason didn't ask where his father had been for the last three months. No one asked.

Tonight, as on most family occasions, Jason's parents avoided looking at each other across the table. With a fork and spoon, Jason's mother moved the food on her plate in circles. She ate very little and hardly spoke except to discuss her favorite television drama with Jason's aunt. They fumed about the villain of the series: an ungrateful son betraying the mother who sacrificed so much for him. Jason caught the sisters glancing at Nahm as they discussed the character.

Nahm ran her fingers across the bottom hem of her dress and brushed something invisible off her lap. She had had to take a little from her savings to buy the outfit but she liked the way the garment's lines appeared to evenly distribute the weight she had gained from her pregnancy.

Jason's aunt didn't ask about the baby.

Neither did Jason's grinning uncle.

During a break between courses, away from the table

in the short hall leading to the bathrooms, Jason pulled his smartphone from his shirt pocket. He showed pictures from the hospital to his cousin and her black husband. The husband gave Jason a congratulatory clap on the back the same way Westerners do in movies. He called Jason lucky.

In the women's restroom, Jason's cousin told Nahm that the newborn—underweight and the color of milk—resembled baby pictures of Jason's younger sister, Ivy. Nahm mentioned that Ivy had promised to visit the hospital, but no one had seen her since a week before the delivery. Nahm filled Ivy's absence at the dinner table between Jason and the family accountant.

Outside, the protesters started to chant: *No to vote. No to vote. No to vote.*

Returning to the banquet table, Jason imagined that one of the voices belonged to his sister. Beyond the walls of the Iron Wok Chef, Ivy stood alongside thousands shouting for the establishment of a People's Council and the end of party elections. She had invited Jason to join the cause. When he admitted he didn't fully understand the fight, Ivy smiled and said, "Good people have an obligation to stand against the tyranny of the majority." Jason didn't ask Ivy how she distinguished bad people from good. He didn't tell her how tired he was of feeling obligated to beliefs that were not his own.

The public dissonance rose above the white noise of the restaurant air conditioners. Only Jason's cousin and her husband turned their heads to the balcony. Twice, a loud pop and boom slapped the windows of the building like thunder. Each time, after a few static seconds, the family continued eating, quieter than before.

As servers brought toothpicks to the table, the family accountant downed his third glass of Scotch, stood, and waddled to the apron of the small karaoke stage. He sang "Ai Piah Cia Eh Yia" two times, stopping often to raise the volume of the speakers over the exclamations of demonstrators.

Jason remembered how his grandmother used to sing the same song while working around the house. Her dry feet resembled crinkled paper and made soft scratches against the bare floors. The gentle shuffling joined her chorus: *Life is like the tide of the sea / We rise and fall by turn.*

Jason wondered what family gatherings might be like if his grandmother were still living. Would she approve of his cousin's African-American husband? Would his grandmother try to look past Nahm's race and economic status to find likenesses?

The accountant's song reminded Nahm of stories Jason told about his grandparents migrating from China to escape the famine. Nahm wondered what Jason's grandparents had envisioned for their descendants in Thailand. Wasn't assimilation with the Siamese a part of their dream? Their goal? Couldn't they have predicted their children's children blending and mixing with other nationalities, cultures, and classes?

Outside, the chants condensed: *No to Vote. No Vote. No Vote.*

Jason and Nahm had been together for more than five years. Ivy had inadvertently introduced them. At least four times a week, Ivy stopped at Nahm's cart to buy mango and sticky rice before entering Kaidee Inter Auto Parts. Ivy always spoke to Nahm, and eventually the pair became friends. Sometimes Ivy would come outside of her family's office building just to talk or rant about the government, the lack of accountability and the failing democracy. Nahm didn't have an interest in politics. No matter who stood in charge, it never seemed to improve the quality of life for her parents. Nahm would listen, annoyed but appreciative of Ivy's sincerity.

One late afternoon, Ivy called the family's office at Kaidee. Sick in bed, she asked Jason to bring her mango from the canopied cart downstairs from his office.

Outside the building near the revolving doors, Nahm seemed preoccupied with the telephone wires above. She bagged the rice, fruit slices, sugar, and chili powder, and bound them with a rubber band without looking down from the nests of thick black cables. Jason asked what she saw, and she replied openly, "I'm thinking about the messages going over my head. I'm trying to imagine the senders and receivers." Then she looked Jason in the eyes and held out her hand. "Thirty baht."

Although Jason passed her every day to enter work at his parents' company, he would later admit that he had never noticed Nahm until he visited the cart for Ivy. Jason abhorred sweet foods, but he began stopping to buy mango regularly. Eventually, Nahm started to notice how often he visited her cart and how long he stayed to chat. She confronted him. She asked if he would ever court someone whose family made little money.

"If I like them," he said, "yes."

She asked him why.

Jason squinted, thinking. He remembered a Chinese New Year dinner with his family when he was younger. He recalled the way his mother never let her gaze linger past the center of the tabletop, and how she didn't allow herself to stare at the empty place setting where her husband should be.

"I don't ever want to settle with someone I can't look in the eyes," he said.

She frowned, and he asked if he could meet her when she wasn't working.

Nahm said yes, but added, "I'm not interested in becoming a mistress."

No Vote. No Vote. No Vote. No Vote.

Nahm was a mother now, and she had hoped to finally receive acceptance from Jason's mother and father, not because she needed their validation but because she wanted her daughter to know two sets of grandparents. Nahm had hoped things might be different if the child did not have a dark complexion. She had found traditional approaches online that assured her baby would be born fair skinned. Every day for nine weeks she boiled saffron strands in milk and added a little sugar. She stained the corners of her mouth orange eating a hundred carrots and pomegranates. Even Nahm's father had recommended a chemical supplement he overheard two passengers debating in the back of his tuk-tuk.

Jason's parents still hadn't visited their grandchild in the hospital.

They never spoke of the baby.

No Vote. No Vote.

The family accountant finished. He returned to the table, and everyone clapped politely. Jason and Nahm rose from their seats.

Jason apologized for having to leave early but did not offer a reason for departing. Later, he would call his cousin to explain—Nahm had to return to the hospital for the baby's feeding. On the phone, Jason would invite his cousin and his uncle—her father—to come see the baby.

They would come, because they wanted to.

Nahm and Jason glimpsed themselves in the mirrors behind the karaoke platform. They looked bigger. Standing, their reflection became a part of the mountain mural; their heads among the painted peaks seemed to rise from grey crags.

Nahm pressed her palms together. She gave seven small bows, one for each person still seated at the table. Then it was Jason's turn to bend in reverence, but he didn't. Jason's aunt glared disapprovingly. The family accountant fiddled nervously with the band on his wristwatch.

No Vote. No Vote. No Vote. No.

Before telling his parents about his relationship with Nahm, Jason had asked his uncle how he thought they might react.

"My sister will not be pleased and neither will your father," his uncle had said. "Maybe if this girl were at least half Chinese or high-society Thai."

His uncle asked what they shared in common.

Jason explained that he and Nahm both wanted the same thing: a life in which the only responsibilities were to those they served willingly.

"We both want a choice in what governs us."

Jason reached for Nahm's hand.

Nahm clasped her fingers with his.

Jason nodded in the direction of his uncle and cousin, and they nodded back in recognition. His cousin's husband waved farewell.

Jason and Nahm strode away from the table. Before disappearing beyond the crimson archway, Nahm smiled at the fake snarling dragons scowling down at her.

Outside, in the heat, Ivy and the sweating crowds raised their voices louder.

Jason's father and mother ignored the growing discord. They pretended to be too interested in the remains on their plates to notice the cries for more or their son's waning shadow as he moved further away.

(NO SUBJECT)

To:

Cc/Bcc, From:

Subject:

Pele the Goddess of Volcanoes passed away on Monday at my mom and dad's place. I found her in that armoire you bought me a year ago on our fifth anniversary. Pele had curled herself at the back of an open, empty drawer. When I reached in to pull her out, I discovered a photograph pinned between her furry spine and the rear wall of the wardrobe. It's the picture of you and me in the elevator, the picture you cropped into the meme that made me Internet famous. I put it aside to deal with later. I had Pele's body frozen and made preparations to have her cremated.

On Friday, my sister Jena flew in from Kahului. My other sisters couldn't be bothered to come. I picked up Jena at Lihue

Airport and we drove straight to the veterinary hospital. We waited silently in the main lobby while an assistant clinician fetched the corpse. A sorry-looking boy in wrinkled scrubs and blackened sandals shuffled up to me with a large cardboard box that read, *Love + Remembrance. Kaumuduli'i Animal Clinic.* The kid stared at me through the bangs of his shaggy hair, scanning my face, trying to remember where he had seen me before. I turned away. I avoid people under thirty because my eyes betray me. They say, *Yes, I'm the one from that image in the comments section of viral videos, the one from that pic sent to friends in text messages about getting blackout drunk, the one from that meme that became so hugely popular a major Korean pop star had it printed on a T-shirt and wore it during a performance on an American music awards show, yes, that one.*

My sister collected the box and set it on one of the waiting room benches. She pulled back the folded flaps and inside the box Pele rested, wrapped in a pink plastic biohazard bag. The box resembled the drawer of the armoire in width and depth. Again, I reached in for Pele. I pulled open the mouth of the bag and Pele's swollen, frosted eyes stared up at me. Her whiskers clung to the sides of her muzzle, and clumps of sparkling ice covered the purple tongue pushed past her dingy fangs.

Pele the Goddess was orange. Do you remember? She used to be the color of hot lava, the color of fire. A bounding flame, a roaming flame, Pele would vanish for weeks and return suddenly. Suddenly, a tiny blaze appears on your chest in the dark as you fall asleep alone in bed; a tiny blaze you thought was lost creeps out from under a couch or table or out of an open armoire. Death transmutes us. She used to be orange. She used to make heat. Bleached by the white cold of fatality and a deep freezer, Pele became a distant yellow.

My mother had gone ahead to the temple. She had been waiting with a Theravada monk and the technician who would return Pele's remains to fire. Hidden behind a large prayer hall, the small concrete structure that housed the crematorium could only be identified by the long rust-spotted pipe jutting out from its terracotta roof tiles. Inside the cramped space, Jena, Mom, the monk, and I watched quietly as the technician worked. He laid a square of clean linen over the surface of a medical table and pulled on a pair of latex gloves. He removed Pele from the packaging, placed her on the cloth, and then grabbed a permanent marker from a bin on a nearby shelf. On the fabric, the technician scribbled words and characters I could not understand. Next to Pele's corpse sat a bundle of incense sticks and a small clay bowl of magenta orchid petals. He instructed my mother, Jena, and me to step toward the table. He told us to sprinkle the petals over Pele. With a lighter he lit three incense sticks and handed one to each of us. The monk cleared his throat and asked everyone to lower their heads. I pressed my palms together, trapping the thin smoldering stick between my index fingers. I bent my neck forward and raised my prayer hands. My lips kissed my thumbs and I listened to the monk incant scriptures from the Pāli Canon. His voice covered me like the fragrant smoke.

While the monk chanted, I thought about Pele. I remembered her as a hungry stray stalking you and me and our bag of fresh salmon through the open market near the house we used to rent together. I remembered her sitting like Buddha by our patio window, scratching her folded ears as she contemplated the mysteries of the universe.

A smartphone chimed through my reflection. The technician's ringtone sang in the breast pocket of his short-sleeved Oxford. I waited for him to silence the device. I waited for him to answer it. When he didn't, I erupted at him. The monk had stood between the technician and me. I nearly pushed the holy man to the ground as I reached for the front of the technician's shirt. The phone continued ringing under my shouts. Cornered against the table where Pele's carcass lay, the technician failed to understand why I was attacking him. Jena and my mother grabbed me. Someone pulled my arms behind me. Another tugged at my waist. They dragged me outside as I cursed the technician for being thoughtless, for not seeing the gravity of Pele's death. In my explosion the incense fell to the floor. I had stomped the sticks to dust. The black ash stained the tiles of the crematorium.

Beside the prayer hall, I bent over and retched onto the roots of a shrub. My mother rubbed my back while Jena stood over me, searching her purse for a wet wipe. Jena passed me a single moist napkin. She observed me while I cleaned my mouth and face. Her brow furrowed with concern, and she asked, "Is this just about the cat?"

I swatted my sister's eyes, scratching the top of her left cheek. She staggered, perhaps more from shock than the force of my slap. The red claw marks flushed with blood.

In response, Jena began to scream. She told me things about myself: how I make myself impossible to love, how I had successfully alienated the last sister willing to talk to me, how I had managed to lose everyone's respect, how I had managed to lose you, how I couldn't take care of you or myself or a cat, how I couldn't take care of anything. Jena called Mom an enabler and then demanded my mother's car keys. Jena would drive herself to our parents' house. Dad would be there because he hadn't seen the point in attending Pele's cremation. Jena would explain to Dad what had happened, and he'd remind Jena that he had warned her not to come. He'd drive her to the airport so she could catch an earlier flight. Before storming away, Jena said that by choosing to be a fuck-up I had prompted you to upload and caption that unflattering photo of me inebriated in an elevator.

My mother took my shaking hands into hers. In her calmest voice she asked me if I had been taking the Seroquel. I lied and said yes because I didn't want the anger to be explained with chemistry. I wanted what I felt to swallow and scorch the Earth. Looking down at my mother's fingers clasped with mine, I imagined the specks of Jena's flesh trapped under my nails.

Mom returned to the crematorium alone to apologize. She saw the technician slide Pele into the furnace. Mom chose a beautiful urn decorated with a hundred dharma wheels and lotus patterns. Now the urn sits on the cheap plywood desk in my room and behind it, tacked to an otherwise empty corkboard, is the 4x6 photo of you and me.

In the picture, the mirrors and fake wood panels bounce the camera flash. Light swallows our shadows. Your pajamas are royal blue, an honest color, and it looks good on you. I have a lime-green tank top and it almost matches the neon glow necklace hovering over my collarbones.

I appear to be enjoying myself. My open mouth reveals rows of crooked teeth. I make sure to cover my teeth when I talk to people now. You've pursed your lips into a wry half-smile. Whatever has caused me to guffaw you don't find as funny. Or maybe you did and you've just stopped laughing. I'm tired, shiny with sweat. My head leans back against your shoulder. Hair sticks to my red face. You spread the digits of your right hand to grip my naked arm, pressing so firmly the tips of your fingers turn white. My eyes are shut. You keep me on my feet. Your eyes, open and ready, wait for my next blinding burst and the subsequent flash of cameras.

What should I do with this grainy, fading moment? I could scan it and put it online, snap a picture of this picture and post it to social media, tag us forever, turn our mistakes into ghosts haunting the invisible webs moving between us.

Maybe this picture of us on the elevator should stay lost in a dresser drawer. I wish I could do the same with others, remove them from digital walls and tuck them somewhere I might forget them.

Everywhere I go, there is a screen and Wi-Fi. How do I move on when my history is mobile? How do I get past all the ways I've hurt people when the past moves with me?

You can't answer these questions, so I will never send this email. I will destroy this picture of us, douse the photo in something 80-proof and set fire to it in a steel trash bin in my parents' yard. I'll have the half-smile then. As the flames erase me and you and the elevator, it will be a kind of death. I will be transmuted. The ashes from this image of me will resemble those in Pele's urn; we will be siblings.

When I was a child, my mother told me stories about Kaʻōhelo, Pele's mortal sister. Kaʻōhelo was so favored by Pele that the goddess captured Kaʻōhelo's spirit in a burning bush that could withstand the heat of magma. My mother told me whenever you see an ʻōhelo ʻai shrub reaching out from lava flows, it is Kaʻōhelo. For Kaʻōhelo, one life ended and she received another. Maybe in the ashes of the elevator photograph I could find an impossible new life and grow out from underneath devastation and extrusive rock. I could have a life that is a mature shade of green and yields fruit.

Standing over the flames, I will curl my toes and root the heels of my bare feet into the warm, muddy sward. The Internet will vanish into smoke. I can be instant. It will be so cathartic I won't care that my mother might be watching from a kitchen window and that she might start worrying again. I won't think about being broke and not having found another job. I'll think of Pele and cleansing fire, and the heat rising from the short cylinder might remind me that there is a world of things I can end and begin again.

#COOKIEMONSTER

COOKIE MONSTER:

MAID WATCHES MINOR CHOKE TO DEATH ON OREO

<www.crimelinx.com/2011/9-odd-arrests>

February 14, 2011 5:53 p.m.

By Peter Commons

In Claudia, Texas, a housekeeper, Xiaoting "Rosa" Chen, 26, faces manslaughter charges for the death of James Hurtado, 16.

On January 26, 2011, police responded to a 911 call from the residence where Chen served as a live-in maid. On arrival, law enforcement found Chen waiting in the front yard. According to the police report, Chen showed a calm demeanor as she led officers inside the home.

The body of James Hurtado was discovered in the kitchen. His breathing appeared to have been obstructed while eating a black and white sandwich cookie. Chen admitted she saw Hurtado choking and did nothing to save him. Officers took Chen into custody. Hurtado's father and mother were away for the evening. Police notified the parents of their son's death.

The coroner revealed that Hurtado had been dead from asphyxiation for more than an hour before Chen dialed 911. Authorities arrested Chen. She currently awaits trial.

TAGS: Texas, Child Negligence, Manslaughter, Nanny, Rosa Chen, Cookie Monster

Tell us what you think! <u>Leave a comment</u>.

OBITUARIES—JAMES L. HURTADO

<www.claudiaherald.com/obituaries>

Claudia, TX

James Luis Hurtado, 16, passed away Wednesday, January

26, 2011. Born February 14, 1994.

James was an only child to Dr. Edward Hurtado and Texas State Senator Sonia Hurtado. Affectionately known as Big Red by family and friends—for his size and auburn hair—James will be remembered for a personality bigger than his stature. Always active and outgoing, James enjoyed helping others. He attended Claudia High School, serving on the Student Council and playing tight end for the championship football team.

A viewing will be held at Bales Funeral Home on Sunday, January 30, 2011 at 10:30 a.m. A Mass in celebration of James' life will be held at St. Patrick's Cathedral, 412 North Mesa Street on Sunday, January 30, 2011 at 1:00 p.m.

The Hurtado family has established a college scholarship fund in honor of James. In lieu of flowers, donations may be made to The James L. Hurtado Scholarship and sent to Senator Sonia's District Office: 517 North Ochoa Street, Suite 6, El Paso, TX 79901. For online condolences, please visit:

www.balesfuneralhome.com.

Published in the Claudia Herald on January 28, 2011

<www.twitter.com/SenSoniaHurtado/status/301843240>

March 12, 2011

Thank you for the outpouring of support. We were blessed to be James' parents. Ed & I will carry our son's spirit. Pray for justice. #BigRed – 1,203 RETWEETS / 5,222 FAVORITES

THE REAL RED

March 13, 2011

By Gillian – 0 COMMENTS

I've never been a fan of the Hurtado's or their son, Red. The media has sanctified the boy, but believe me, he was awful—God bless the dead. He'd tear through the neighborhood after every football game, revving his truck real loud, blaring music, shouting and hollering. Last year, after he won the State championship, he got blackout-drunk. The Carroway's found him in their garden wearing nothing but a jock strap, his pecker in the dirt beneath Barbara Carroway's chrysanthemums. Oh, and Lord forbid the boy lost a game. One time after a devastating loss to a rival team, he ripped my mailbox right out of the ground, post and all, and tossed it into the street. The boy was scary sometimes, no regard for anything. I had to remind his mother four times before she finally paid to replace my mailbox. Imagine it. I'm the head of the Homeowner's Association and I have to ask my neighbor to reign in their son.

Don't get me wrong, as much as I viewed their son as a menace, I do feel sorry for them. To lose a son that way—choking to death on a cookie. Jesus weeps, it's so embarrassing. And that idiot housekeeper of theirs just standing there doing nothing. I always thought that girl was a little slow. You could barely talk to her without her staring off at nothing. She always appeared distant and jumpy, like she was on drugs or something.

Anyway, the whole thing is dreadful for everyone. The annual block party for the Homeowner's Association was scheduled for next week. You think anyone feels like celebrating? It'd be inappropriate. Months of planning have just evaporated. I can't get a deposit back on the inflatable castle I reserved or the henna tattoo artist I booked. My husband and his Bluegrass band had agreed to play. People rarely think about how tragedies like this affect an entire community. The whole neighborhood is mournful and glum.

And since the bigger news outlets have got a hold of the story, it's been a nightmare, especially on my property. I've had broadcasters trouncing through my front yard. Network news vans parked along the cul-de-sac like a pioneer caravan, cluttering the road—I can barely get out of the driveway. A few of the television anchors have even knocked on my door to ask if they could use a bathroom. They're all vying to get a glimpse of Sonya or Edward as they leave and enter their house. They rush them for a statement.

I've been over to see them a couple times. I baked them one of my famous Linzer tortes, I told them God has a plan for us all and God must have needed Red to come home sooner than expected. I told them if they needed anything I'd be right next door. Neither of them offered me a single thank you. I know they're hurting, but no wonder their boy was so rude. They never came by when my aunt died last fall. The Hurtado's knew about her passing and I didn't receive so much as a call or card. Not a single condolence. But, I'll continue to be as good a neighbor as I can. I'll keep them in my thoughts and continue praying justice is served.

A full-time mother and housewife in love with vintage fashion and reality TV. I cultivate this online space for women looking for creative approaches to homemaking. On this blog I share recipes, parenting advice and other reflections. Be sure to sign up for my weekly newsletter so you won't miss future posts and updates!

WHO WATCHES OUR CHILDREN?

<www.nycourier.com/2012/06/10/opinion/who-watches-our-children.html>

June 10, 2012

By Donna G. Parkinson

Xiaoting Chen's trial will begin in a few weeks. Chen served as a housekeeper and was the only legal adult in the residence of James Hurtado at the time of his death. Chen stood in a position of temporary caregiver to James Hurtado. She admitted to watching Hurtado choke to death without attempting to save him, and that failure to act and perform her duty is criminal.

"It would be comparable to a lifeguard on duty who refuses to save a drowning person," said Patricia Rebollar, Assistant Attorney General and lead prosecutor in the trial against Chen. Another example can be found in R v. Adomako, 1994, in which a doctor failed to notice that a patient's oxygen supply had disconnected, and the patient died during the operation. The existence of the duty is what's essential here since the law does not recognize that an ordinary person has any obligation to aid or rescue another in distress. One can also be charged in cases of willful blindness, in which the defendant intentionally puts him or herself into a position where they would be unaware of facts that would hold them liable, like if Chen had left the room while Hurtado choked to death.

Rosa Chen's silence magnifies her behavior. She is often seen taking notes, pressing her nose to a legal pad as she scribbles Chinese characters, seemingly uninterested in the events unfolding around her. She appears unreadable—a tinier, angrier Lucy Liu. There is no indication that Chen has received any coaching on courtroom conduct from her counsel.

Some might view her muteness as a smart move. Chen's limited English could allow the prosecution to manipulate or lead her answers. However, for many her silence has been viewed as an admission of guilt.

ADD A COMMENT...

COMMENTS (3):

LIVY BAL (PLYMOUTH, OHIO)—*She already admitted to police that she watched this kid die and did nothing. Why are we even having a trial?*

JENA KUHIO (KAHULUI, HAWAII)—*Her confession might have been forced. She isn't a native English speaker. She might not have understood what the police were even saying.*

ANGELA DAVIS (FRESNO, CALIFORNIA)—*To the Hurtado family, I am sorry for the loss of your son James. My thoughts are still with you during this trial. Praying for justice. #BigRed #cookiemonster*

THE DEFENSE IS FAILING CHEN

<www.dallastribune.com/2012/07/10/opinion/the-defense-is-failing-chen-issue.html>

July 10, 2012

By Megan C. Nguyen

Rosa Chen's defense took a hard hit yesterday. State prosecutors revealed that police discovered nude photos of Chen on James Hurtado's mobile phone. The prosecution will use these pictures to establish adequate cause for murder, and the public defender's office does not look prepared for this fight.

Chen was originally charged with criminally negligent manslaughter. However, the prosecution has pushed for second-degree murder. In their estimation, her hesitation to save Hurtado was willful. Prosecutors argue that Chen's position warrants criminal liability and that she had motive to kill. New allegations, supported by the discovery of the pictures on Hurtado's mobile phone, help invent a scenario in which her failure to save Hurtado becomes the act of a jealous sexual aggressor.

The testimony from Jill Ortega, Hurtado's girlfriend at the time of his death, has helped state attorneys build a case that presents James Hurtado as a victim of statutory rape. One of Hurtado's former football teammates corroborated this claim by telling the court that Hurtado had "bragged" about having slept with his maid, Chen. According to these statements, it can be inferred that Hurtado, having just started dating Ortega, tried to refuse Chen's sexual advances, and that Chen, feeling rejected and possibly worried about being unveiled as a sex offender, allowed Hurtado to choke to death.

The evidence, circumstantial and dependent on speculation, is no less of a threat to Chen's acquittal. The defendant's legal counsel has not provided an alternate theory, nor do they intend to use these nude photos to their advantage. Can a 5'3" woman weighing little more than 108 pounds rape a boy 6'3" and 236 pounds? The point is not to launch a discourse about the definition of rape, but to play on common misconceptions about gender and power. The defense can utilize the same stratagem employed by the prosecution, passive suggestion, posing questions to the jury that lead them to the conclusions benefiting one's case.

Would Chen, the niece of one of China's preeminent human rights attorneys, Chen, the only living child of a woman who died during a forced abortion, Chen, who was still in the process of applying for asylum at the time of her arrest, risk everything to seduce a teenage boy? Isn't it more likely that Hurtado abused Chen's resident status and employment position to coerce her into a sexual relationship? What about rumors that James had a history of sexual assault? Was Chen made to take these photos? If so, what obligation would Chen have to rescue someone who had sexually assaulted her? These are not defamations. These are questions the defense should be asking.

Chen's attorneys are overconfident in the prosecution's inability to prove their case beyond a reasonable doubt. Her lawyers chose not to give an opening statement. They do not intend to submit a single piece of evidence or call a single witness, ultimately leaving jurors with only one version of the incident. The jury will not be given an opportunity to hear Chen's side of the story. They will not have a chance to hear her voice at all. She will not take the stand or go under oath.

In a trial like this, appearance can play a big factor in the jury's decision. Journalists and law bloggers have noted that Chen comes across as inscrutable, potentially summoning negative Western perceptions of East Asia. Indeed, many media outlets have already used words like unreadable, mysterious, and cold to describe the defendant. Her barbed gaze seems to invite a bevy of comparisons to martial-arts movie villainesses.

These depictions are compounded by Senator Sonia Hurtado's successful campaign against Chen, which has garnered hundreds of thousands of supporters online and prompted #BigRed support tees, hats, and rubber bracelets. Senator Sonia Hurtado never goes too long without reminding her followers to "Pray for

Justice." She appears to be slipping out of the courtroom every hour to live-tweet the proceedings and offer commentary on the defendant's movements. The Senator's 140-character blasts are often reminiscent of the xenophobia seen during America's obsession with the Yellow Peril.

This serves as an example of what the defense faces. There is no way to separate the opinions flooding the vast expanse of digital media from the truth, whatever it might be. Innocent until proven guilty is an ideal. Rosa Chen cannot receive a fair trial free of the influence of Senator Hurtado's pleas across social media, free of the influence of news camera clips of a puffy-eyed Dr. Edward Hurtado still mourning the death of his son.

Chen's lawyers need to be aware of the scope of what their client contends with. They need to be prepared for a real fight. Rosa Chen is not facing a jury of her peers. None of the jurors are Asian American, and most are upper middle class. The defense attorneys cannot hope for a fair ruling. The defense has to be proactive in order to overturn the verdict that has already been read during Chen's trial by Twitter. The defense needs to be reminded that their client will have to be proven innocent. They need to acknowledge that for most of the jurors and most of the public, Xiaoting Chen is "the Cookie Monster," and she was guilty before she stepped into the courtroom.

Megan C. Nguyen is a lawyer, author, and MSNBC News legal analyst.

ADD A COMMENT...

COMMENTS (17):

LIVY BAL (PLYMOUTH, OHIO)—*Has it occurred to the author that perhaps people are saying Chen is cold because she is?*

RICHARD MATTHEWS (EL PASO, TEXAS)—*Maybe the defense fails Chen because they know she's guilty.*

SILVIA ANNAN (CLAUDIA, TEXAS)—*Do you need to have the law explained to you? Irregardless of whether or not the lawyers think she is guilty they have an obligation to defend their client to the best of their ability.*

LIVY BAL (PLYMOUTH, OHIO)—*Do you need someone to explain how "irregradless" is not a word?*

PHILLIP DAWKINS (BURLINGTON, VERMONT)—*To which xenophobic tweets does the writer refer?*

SAM BREVARD (RENO, NEVADA)—*Sonia Hurtado called Chen "sneaky" and "untrustworthy," and people got all butt hurt about it. The tweets have been removed. If someone were responsible for my son's death I'd probably say much worse.*

MIKE DONALD (DALLAS, TEXAS)—*How limited is her English if she's reading and filling out asylum forms? o_o*

BETH GOPIN (NEW YORK CITY, NEW YORK)—*Senator Hurtado is an immigration lawyer. I'm sure she had been helping Chen before all this happened. You don't need to speak perfect English to apply for asylum.*

REBECCA ANNAN (CLAUDIA, TEXAS)—*(A moderator removed this comment because it did not abide by our community standards.)*

JOHNATHAN REKDALL (KANSAS CITY, MISSOURI)—*Um...Rumors of sexual assault? How is that not slander?*

SILVIA ANNAN (CLAUDIA, TEXAS)—*It isn't slander if it's true. <http://www.changers.org/petitions/governor-free-rosa-chen>*

RICHARD MATTHEWS (EL PASO, TEXAS)—*So, this chick starts a petition asking Governor Russ Coldwell to release Chen because she claims she was sexually assaulted by this kid a year earlier? Does that even make sense?*

ROB THOMAS (FLORENCE, SOUTH CAROLINA)—*1. There's zero way to prove that Hurtado forced himself on his teacher. 2. She's a teacher!*

How did she let that even happen? 3. What does it have to do with Chen's case?

SILVIA ANNAN (CLAUDIA, TEXAS)—*It establishes a pattern!!! It has everything to do with Chen's case!*

JOHNATHAN REKDALL (KANSAS CITY, MISSOURI)—*EXACTLY, Rob! Even if what Rebecca Annan says is true, how is it relevant to this? And why didn't Rebecca Annan come forward before this? Seems like she's just after the spotlight.*

SILVIA ANNAN (CLAUDIA, TEXAS)—*Johnathan, you have no idea how powerful the Hurtado family is in Claudia? Rebecca feared coming forward because she knew there'd be assholes like you dismissing her as some kind of opportunist. After it happened she refused to tell anyone. She quit her job at Claudia High and started at another school the following year. When she saw what was happening she felt she had to come forward to help Chen.*

JOHNATHAN REKDALL (KANSAS CITY, MISSOURI)—*You know, name-calling doesn't really help your argument, and again, even if she went to the police and filled a report, the suspect is dead. There is no way of proving that James did what she said. So it has no bearing on this trial. The only pattern being established is that he possibly had a thing for older women.*

Aaron Q. Martinez

July 12, 2012

People have already made up their mind by this point. They've read an article or a blog post or a message board or a feed, they've talked to someone who knows someone else and are one-hundred percent sure about the events that occurred between two people and zero witnesses. They can cite sources and fight about it on social media and feel safe in their righteousness because they're removed from the situation—it doesn't affect them personally. It doesn't really matter what I say about Rebecca Annan, right, or how it relates to what happened to that girl, Rosa Chen?

I'm sorry. I'm not trying to be antagonistic. I'm just tired of the pretense. People look for evidence to support the narrative that makes the most sense to them. Since her first day at school, Rebecca kept mostly to herself. She was clearly a dedicated educator. She viewed teaching as a vocation, not a job. She always smiled, never complained like the rest of us. She didn't join in any of the teachers' lounge gossip, although she would nod along in agreement to something funny occasionally.

But then, after James Hurtado joined one of her history classes, Rebecca came to school one day looking fearful. She was jumpy and stammering. Shortly after that, she called in sick for a number of weeks. I had to cover some of her sections for the remainder of the semester. Our principal said Rebecca had mono, and I didn't think much about it.

Rebecca returned the following semester. Rebecca didn't smile anymore. She had visibly stopped taking care of herself, and there were complaints from students about her body odor. Something had obviously upset her.

James died at the end of January, and Rebecca resigned and moved away about a month later. Before she left, she'd become increasingly irritable and seemingly more distracted. Her teaching suffered.

I didn't hear the rumors about James Hurtado until the following fall. There are two different narratives, of course, one in which Rebecca is the victim and another in which she is the predator. So I'll repeat what I've told all the reporters. I don't know for certain what occurred between Rebecca Annan and James Hurtado. I have an opinion about what happened, a conclusion I've drawn based on my on limited perceptions and experiences.

And so does everyone else.

CHEN PLEADS GUILTY AND RECEIVES A REDUCED SENTENCE

<http://hosted.associatedpress.org/stories/A/XIAOTING_CHEN_TRIAL?SITE>

July 15, 2012 11:53 p.m. EDT

By Todd Cox, *Associated Press*

Claudia, TX—The week-long trial of Xiaoting Chen came to a conclusion Saturday in a Hulsey County courtroom. Chen agreed to a last-minute plea bargain for a second-degree murder charge and twenty-five years in prison without parole.

Patricia Rebollar, Assistant Attorney General and lead prosecutor in the case, shared that she was pleased with the outcome.

"This was a heinous crime. We hope the Hurtado family can rest easier, knowing someone has been held accountable for the death of their beloved son," said Rebollar.

Before delivering the sentence, Judge Jane Cooper-Thomas addressed Chen personally.

"You were entrusted with the care of a young man with a bright future," Cooper-Thomas said. "Arizona State University had offered him a football scholarship. He planned to study criminology. James Hurtado could have done great things. He could have brought more joy to his family, friends, and the world. Unfortunately, he is not here today. You had a responsibility to that young man, and you failed him."

Prosecutors claim that Chen allowed James Hurtado to choke to death. They believe the incident was motivated by a secret sexual relationship with the minor.

During the delivery of the defense's closing arguments, Chen's lead attorney, Roman Alfred, said, "It is beyond reasonable comprehension that Rosa Chen could have willfully allowed this boy to die."

"The State would have you believe that Rosa was engaged in a sexual relationship with this young man, and that her inaction was spurred by malice. There is no real evidence to prove this," Alfred told jurors during his closing argument. "There are no monsters in this case. Rosa Chen was simply in a state of shock.

Such a harsh sentence would not only be unfair, it would set an awful precedent for this community by saying that we punish people for being afraid." Alfred asked jurors to set aside biases and use common sense before making their decision. However, late Friday evening, the defense came to prosecutors and drafted a new plea deal.

Chen had been silent during much of the week's proceedings, but Saturday morning, when asked if she would like to make a statement before receiving her sentence, Chen addressed the courtroom for the first time.

Senator Sonia Hurtado became visibly upset after Chen spoke. She wept softly during the sentencing. Her husband, Dr. Edward Hurtado, wrapped an arm around her shoulders, attempting to console her. He also shed many tears. Senator Hurtado, who has been very outspoken during the trial, appeared to be at a loss for words. She and her husband refused to speak to reporters as they left the courthouse.

"We have justice at cost to others," Chen said. "For what you lose, I am sorry, Mrs. Hurtado. Mr. Hurtado, I am sorry for your pain. I did not save your son. I could not make me save him. Now you will have some justice, and I have mine."

TWIN PILGRIMS

A few hundred seconds before the next giant leap for mankind, Livy comes home weary from Sacramento. You try to ignore the heavy thud of Livy's duffle bag on the rug in the front hallway, Livy's slogging steps to the kitchen, the creak and slam of the refrigerator door, and her grumbling about a stench pervading the house.

So much noise.

You don't need to ask if Livy and her former fiancé reconciled over the weekend. They didn't. You know this, not because you and Livy share an intuitive bond like some other twins, but because you still have enough reason to recognize the only solution to the couple's separation.

But Livy won't leave Plymouth because she can't leave you.

Livy shifts and clangs the dirty cast-iron pots abandoned in the sink two nights earlier, remnants of your failed attempt to recreate Mom's sweet plantain with spicy spinach stew.

Livy exhales loudly before entering the living room. She finds you. You've curled on the couch in a fetal position. Livy doesn't ask why you didn't pick her up from the airport. If she did ask, you would motion to the smartphone in your hand and remind Livy of the occasion—the crew of the Harbinger 1 had scheduled to land three hours ago. You would have had plenty of time to drive to the airport to collect Livy. The unpredictability of space travel is not your fault.

On the four-inch screen, pink sand begins to swirl beneath the blast of thrusters. Livy pushes your feet off the cushions and sits down. She sniffs the air. "Something's funky in here, Geri." The legs of the landing module unfold from the bottom of the carriage. "How long have those pots been sitting in the sink?" The spaceship sinks toward a shallow red basin. "Geri, where is Pocky? Did you leave him outside? Deoiridh?"

You shush Livy.

So much noise.

Livy rises from the sofa. "Geri, where is my dog?"

I hear panic grip Livy's throat.

Pocky had originally belonged to you. You got him shortly after learning that Mom had amyotrophic lateral sclerosis. Because you didn't have the same obligations as other siblings—no mortgage or children—you volunteered to move back to Plymouth to help Livy care for Mom. Livy had suggested an affordable hospice, but you refused. To demonstrate your commitment to staying, you adopted a three-month-old puppy, a small brown mutt, part poodle and Chihuahua, from the Plymouth animal shelter.

I wanted to make it work. I thought it could be a new beginning for Mom and me.

Be honest with yourself. Your concern for Mom was not the impetus for your return home. You had lost your job teaching primary school children in India.

I didn't lose anything. I had written a few letters to the administration of the English language center, offering suggestions on how they could improve, and soon after, they fired me for repeated dress code infractions and student complaints. They had obviously been looking for a reason to get rid of me for months.

Without the school sponsoring your visa and no other work opportunities immediately available, you decided it might be a good time to finally return home. You rationalized the move back as an opportunity to start a new chapter in the place your story began. You viewed caring for Mom as a kind of penance for the years you had been gone.

After coming back to Plymouth, Livy recommended you for a page position at the local college library where she served as a circulation coordinator.

You didn't work well with most of your co-workers.

My supervisor—Eric or Derrick something—was unbearable, one of those people who yammer on about how much they like to read but can only list big names in contemporary American pop fiction. He'd recount these trite plotlines whenever we worked the circulation desk together, and I couldn't feign interest.

Don't glance over your own faults. Your tardiness became an issue.

I had trusted Livy to wake me up. I have trouble rising on my own. When I was still living in India, I had to pay neighborhood kids in Chennai to shout outside my window in the morning.

You had only worked at the library for three months before you were fired for two absences in one week.

I'm only surprised Derrick or Eric hadn't done it sooner. Even when I did show up I spent most of my time hiding among the stacks, rereading Hughes, Baldwin, and Wright. I caught up on Sebald, Gombrowicz, Goethe, and Plenzdorf, and some other recommendations I had overheard a group of Berlin street artists discussing during my stay at a hostel in Nairobi.

Sometimes, I'd abandon shelving books and sneak to a secluded study carrel to watch online livestreams from the International Space Exploration Coordination Group's simulation outposts in New Mexico and Antarctica. Of those twenty-four candidates chosen for the trials to see who would be among the first human settlers on Mars, three had been selected from open applicants. I wasn't one of them. I had applied two years earlier but never received a response.

Whenever you experience a significant rejection, you recall your failure to become an astronaut. At the time you applied, you were your best self, physically and mentally. You had found a healthy balance between diet, exercise, and

Lexapro. You had completed the Queenstown International Marathon and an equally grueling Vipassana retreat in Myanmar that involved ten days of monastic living, meditation, and embracing a silence you thought helped prepare you for the quiet void of space.

Instead of clearing out your cubby at the library and saying goodbye to your co-workers, you took a long walk through downtown Plymouth and pondered reasons the International Space Exploration Coordination Group (ISECG) might have overlooked you. While considering what the scientists and recruiters must have seen or not seen in your application, you noticed your reflection in a shop window.

Earlier that morning, you had wrapped your hair in one of Mom's Kente cloth headscarves, and you didn't realize how much the orange clashed with your bright green skinny jeans. A line of dried toothpaste at the side of your mouth showed that in your rush to get to the library an hour late, you had forgotten to wipe your face after brushing your teeth.

You had left the top buttons of your sky-blue blouse unclasped. You ran a finger across your prominent collarbones and you thought, *I'm getting so fat here, pie-for-breakfast fat, cake-on-the-nightstand fat.*

You sighed. You didn't feel ready to return home to have to listen to Mom's crying, Livy's lecturing, and Pocky's incessant yapping. *So much noise.* You searched for a place to sit and think. You saw a vacant wrought-iron bench outside the only coffee shop in town. You sat and watched the cars pass through the intersection of Fourth and Main. You frowned at the succession of sport utility vehicles and minivans. You scoffed at the sincerity of the bumper stickers and the window decals of stick-figure families—stick men, stick women, and children and dogs and cats, signaling to other drivers that a more fulfilled person steers this vehicle.

You looked up and thanked the universe for making you the kind of person whose spirituality, wit, and politics couldn't be summarized by glossy vinyl clichés daring other motorists to disagree.

You thought, What am I doing here?

While sitting on that bench, I remembered a conversation I had had with Livy the day I arrived from India to move in with Mom.

Livy and I had been standing in front of that same coffee shop.

Livy inhaled deeply and said, "I love this café."

I smiled and said, Yes, if you squint hard enough you can almost imagine you're somewhere else.

Livy didn't laugh. She stared at me curiously, parsing what I had said.

Taking a sip from my cup, I swallowed the botched espresso along with my desire to complain to the barista about how the drink smelled and tasted like burnt paper.

Livy continued, "I'm so glad to see you again. I can't believe you've finally come home."

"Neither can I," I said.

"I know Plymouth might not be as noteworthy as some of the places you've lived, Geri, but it's growing and changing. Maybe you've been called home to do something meaningful here."

Livy's saccharine tone nearly caused me to choke on my bitter coffee.

I told her that my only priority was taking care of Mom.

Livy changed the subject. "I think we'll be hiring soon at the library, if you're interested."

"Sure, anything works for now," I said.

"And what do you hope to find?"

"Like I said, anything."

"Right," Livy turned away and appeared to nod knowingly at something only she could see. She said, *"Geri, in all this time you've been out searching the world, did you ever find yourself?"*

I scanned the hot black water in my coffee cup for a possible answer to Livy's question.

"Deoiridh, if you don't know what to do, you don't have to figure things out alone."

Then the bells of the Baptist church two blocks away began to chime, indicating the arrival of a new hour, punctuating the end of Livy's sentence and preempting my response.

You rose from the bench outside the coffee shop.

You headed home, still thinking again about Livy's words.

I walked around town for hours trying to decide if I could ever find what I wanted. When I finally returned home, Livy was waiting for me inside, having dinner with Mom. Together they had prepared my favorite meal, sweet plantain and spinach stew—I had never taken the time to learn how to make it myself. Pocky was perched on Livy's knees, poking his snout over the edge of the dining table, yowling endlessly for food. Mom belly-laughed at Pocky's persistence.

You remember what you felt at that moment, looking over the joyful scene?

Jealousy, at Mom and Livy for enjoying themselves so much without me.

And then anger?

Anger because I couldn't understand why I should even care.

Livy asked if I was hungry, and I said no.

She said she had taken Pocky for a walk and given him a bath.

I thanked her.

Later, Mom got tired and had to lie down. She took Pocky to bed with her. Soon we heard Mom's wheezing snores, and then Livy began to scold me. She spoke firmly and calmly, in the same tone I'd heard her employ at the library whenever she had to tell a patron that they had accrued late charges or that they wouldn't be able to graduate if the missing books they'd borrowed were not returned or replaced.

Livy said I needed to be more responsible and think about how my actions affected others. She said it was unfair of me to put her in a position where she must apologize for my behavior. It would be hard enough to care for Mom; Livy couldn't look after me too.

I agreed.

I apologized to Livy, and when she went to use the bathroom before the drive back to her fiancé's apartment, I stole a credit card from her wallet. That evening I searched online for nations with a low cost of living that do not require a tourist visa before entering, and then I booked the cheapest flight I could find to Thailand.

When I landed in Bangkok, I caught a commuter van and then took a ferry to one of the less popular islands.

Days passed before I located a tiny Internet café with a single computer.

I emailed Livy.

I wrote TAKE CARE OF POCKY FOR ME and clicked send.

E-MINUS 60 SECONDS AND COUNTING

Livy exits the rear patio door to search the yard.

She calls for Pocky with nervous shouts.

You want to demand her silence. You want the world to stop in reverence of this moment. You don't understand how anyone could be concerned about locating a dog while humanity pushes its boundaries into the heavens.

Few people share your obsession with the Harbinger 1 mission. You've been disappointed with the lack of media coverage, and surprised you don't overhear people speaking about the colonization of Mars whenever you feel brave enough to venture outside of Mom's house. But you realize most folks tend to focus on what they already know, what affects them directly.

The majority of people are content living predictable lives and have little interest in something that might disrupt the certainty they've cultivated.

Livy is the same way.

If I had to describe her with a single word—reliable. And she has always been more practical than me. As a kid she would turn her side of the bedroom into a veterinary clinic, and I would transform our closet into a rocket ship. I'd imagine flying through space to discover a world where I'd finally feel less alien. In middle school, I'd spend hours reading about ISECG's terraforming orbiter, Gardner 1. Livy became interested in homemaking. I learned everything I could about how Gardner 1's seed probes would provide sustainable food sources for future men and women on Mars. Mom taught Livy how to cook and sew.

Mom and Livy shared a preference for the concrete.

I guess I'm more like Dad.

Mom would talk a lot about Dad. Livy and I never knew him; he died in a car crash in Nairobi just a few weeks before we were born. He had been traveling through rural areas of Kenya collecting data on how family factors affect the mental health of children and the potential for curbing HIV/AIDS using these observations on family dynamics.

Dad met Mom doing similar research in Ghana. She was a university student from Accra, and she had volunteered for the project to receive school credit. They fell in love and Mom returned with Dad, a Dutchman, to the Netherlands. Not long after came my big sister, Joyce. My brothers Joel, Kristopher, and David followed. My older siblings had all reached their early twenties before Dad accepted a tenure-track position teaching African studies at a small liberal arts college in Ohio. And then Livy and I came along. Mom called us the last great surprise Dad ever gave her.

Growing up in Plymouth, you'd often ask Mom what spurred Dad to move from a global city like Amsterdam to a boring little town.

And Mom would say, "As a girl in Accra, somewhere else, like Europe or America, always seemed better and more fascinating. But eventually I realized a place is only as boring as I choose to see it."

You disagreed vehemently. Plymouth's lack of excitement had to be objective. You intended to travel the world like Dad as soon as you became old enough. After high school you made plans to spend a year in the Netherlands living with your older siblings.

Livy stayed in Plymouth and enrolled at the college.

Five years passed before you and Livy saw each other again in person.

Your sister Joyce had asked if you wanted to accompany her and your nephews to Plymouth for Christmas. Uncomfortable pauses, prolonged silences, and passive-aggressive snipes plagued the holiday as the four of you struggled to contain past grievances and reacquaint yourselves with one another. The gift Mom gave to you on Christmas Day embodied her sentiments about your absence: an expensive fountain pen with a card that read, "Write Home More, My Little Pilgrim. – Mom."

You and Livy barely spoke, limiting your conversations to pleasant observations about the food and decorations. The two of you had always had differences, but the physical and emotional distance had become a chasm neither of you cared enough to bridge.

I was glad to return to Holland, but even the Netherlands grew repetitive after a while.

When Europe began to remind you of Plymouth, you looked for somewhere more exciting. You traveled through East Africa before moving on to East Asia. In every country, you made sure to leave the capital cities. You'd hike into the mountains or climb down to the plains. You'd stare out over the grasslands, bays, and oceans, waiting to feel something unexpected. But all you ever felt looking out over all that majesty was emptiness, and you'd think of Mom and Livy and wonder if anything or anyone could make you feel tied to Earth.

After over a decade and two dozen nations, I found myself increasingly disappointed at how often the rural parts of the developing world looked the same—the same fields, the same shacks, the same gutters, grime, dirt, and ditches.

When you ran out of money but couldn't stand to return home to Mom, you found schools eager to hire native English speakers to teach in India. You discovered having light skin and European features caused many employers to mistake you for a tanned white woman, and you quickly learned that by not correcting them you could earn more money than the majority of your darker-skinned colleagues, even despite most of them having higher qualifications. You started straightening your hair regularly; you replaced your glasses with green contact lenses and began omitting certain aspects of your identity. You changed your name to Geri, fretting that foreign employers might mistake the Gaelic name Mom and Dad gave you, Deoiridh, as something other than white.

E-MINUS 30 SECONDS AND COUNTING

The landing module shudders violently. Your stomach churns. Livy enters the house again through the front door as the crew of the Harbinger I approaches the final meters of their descent.

"I can't find him outside. Geri, where is Pocky?"

You remember.

Pocky would not stop barking while Livy was away in Sacramento. His high-pitched yowl reminded you of the strident whistle blasts on your last train ride from Bengaluru to Chennai.

I had spent half a day confined to my first-class sleeper cabin, and whenever I tried to rest, the whistle came blaring through my dreams to startle me awake.

The chirps from your smartphone seemed to make Pocky yelp even louder. Perhaps Pocky knew it was Livy calling. Livy is the only one who calls you now, the only name listed in your contacts.

Your voice cracked as you said, "H-hello?"

"Geri, are you just waking up? It's 10 a.m."

"No." You cleared your throat and told Livy you had just returned from a run.

In the short silence that followed, you knew Livy considered the truth, fact-checking against a mental index of your past transgressions.

Who you are remains in conflict...*with whom I think I ought to be.*

"Geri, do you think you are in a position to sleep in? Don't you think there is something more constructive you could be doing?"

"I thought taking care of my health was constructive."

Livy sighs. "Right, right."

You told Livy you sent some job applications to Columbus and Cleveland before she left.

"Really?"

You told Livy there had been a few nibbles and that you had thought of doing some freelance translations to earn some quick cash.

"What is a nibble?"

You lied and said there were some promising developments.

Livy's voice perked.

"That's good, Geri! Soon you'll be back on your own again... Did you get a chance to look at that split-level I showed you? The one with the portico?"

"I walked past."

"And?"

"It was okay."

"Just okay? I thought it might be the perfect size for you."

"I don't know."

"I've been talking to a realtor and she thinks we could get a pretty great price on Mom's house. You would get enough from the sale to make a down payment on your own place, and probably have enough left over to buy a decent used car. Of course, you wouldn't have to start paying me back for the credit card and flying you home from China until you have a steady job. And you can take your time repaying me for the hospital bills in Shanghai. No hurry."

"Thanks."

"You know, Paul and I could really use the funds from selling the house. It could really help us to get our lives together out here in Cali."

"I suppose so."

"Think about it and we'll talk when I get back, alright?"

"Yeah. We'll talk."

"I should be landing at CVG the day after tomorrow at 4 p.m. I taped my flight itinerary to the fridge. Please make sure you're there to pick me up. Love you, Geri. Hope you're taking good care of Pocky."

The smoke detector began to squeal.

I ended the phone call with Livy without replying and ran to the kitchen.

Grey clouds bellowed from a blackened skillet of charred plantains. Beside the pan, a bubbling pot belched green slime and strings of spinach onto the stovetop and floor.

You really had meant to be better, like other people, like Mom.

Pocky's bark rose above the hiss of oil and fire, the popping stew, and the relentless whine of the smoke alarm.

I stood in the center of the kitchen, and joined the cacophony with my own rabid shouts.

Shut up.

Shut up!

SHUT UP!

You too, stupid little dog.

Shut up...or I'll make you.

E-MINUS 20 SECONDS AND COUNTING

"Seriously, where is Pocky? Is he upstairs?"

Listening to Livy clomp up the steps to the second floor, you think, *I belong on Mars, not here in Plymouth having to answer to my twin.*

Why are you here?

Maybe sharing Mom's attention with five other siblings instilled a need to be noticed and left alone. Maybe these conflicting desires led you abroad to other countries where you could stand out without having to speak.

After you had gotten fired from the library and escaped to Thailand, Livy eventually canceled the credit card you had stolen. You foraged enough freelance work proofreading and copyediting to live month to month. Eventually, you found a job at an English tutoring center sponsored by a university in the small town of Zhuji, China, south of Hangzhou.

A week before I had to arrive in China, I decided to visit Cambodia. I had hoped a trip to Siem Reap might cure my increasing weariness of the world. Among the ruins of its ancient jungle cities, I'd yearned to experience something new and unexpected.

I climbed the steep stairs to the tallest spire at Angkor Wat. Sweating as I shuffled through the dark stone walkways, I came across a pair of golden sculptures of the Buddha and thought about the age of the statues and how far away they stood from everything I had ever known in Plymouth.

I wondered if Mom had thought something similar when she first landed in the Netherlands. Could she or my ancestors have ever conceived what I saw at that moment? Could they have ever predicted their blood moving across the Earth, the sum of their bodies standing in a land so alien to them?

I might as well have been on another planet.

I thought about perspective.

My chest swelled as I considered all I had experienced, and weighed my privilege against pharaohs, emperors, and kings throughout history.

As I prepared to climb back down into the jungle, I noticed a thin, young backpacker swigging the last few ounces of water from a plastic bottle. He resembled an Eastern Christian depiction of Jesus Christ with a blond beard and light eyes. His flaxen hair was pulled into a bun and a folded bandana replaced a crown of thorns.

The young savior finished with the container. He tossed the empty bottle onto a pile of trash pushed into the corner of a thousand-year-old entranceway.

Unacceptable. How could others not respect the gravity of this place? How could they not also feel changed? How could they be so ungrateful? Reprehensible. People can't be allowed to get away with such disrespect. You had to do something.

I followed him as he rushed down the spire steps to join a group of other travelers leaning against a wall built during the Khmer Empire. When he reached his compatriots, he removed a cell phone from his cargo shorts. I moved closer, and when I heard him complain about the lack of connectivity, I yanked the device from his hands.

You became justice.

I squatted to the ground and smashed the phone on a thick forest root.

You became cosmic retribution, the personification of karma and doom.

I yelled for them all to show reverence.

Backpacker Jesus cursed me.

A few of his friends helped pry the cracked phone from my fingers, and the group hurried away.

You stood up. Soaked with perspiration and satisfaction, you smiled at a couple of concerned onlookers. You waved at them and thought, *It's okay. No need to thank me.*

After Cambodia, you arrived in China and lived in Zhuji for a couple of years, then Guangdong for a few months before moving to Hangzhou and finally Shanghai—a louder city.

Livy called you only once in Shanghai.

It was the first time you had heard her speak in years.

You had been asleep when the phone rang. Barely awake, you were initially confused by the sound of a voice so similar to your own glumly repeating your name.

Livy told you that Mom had died.

And you replied that you couldn't make it to the funeral.

Too busy.

"Too busy?"

You ended the call, and kicked out from underneath your goose-feather comforter.

And then you were alone in your pajamas a block from your apartment, strolling a crowded stretch of Nanjing Road.

So much noise.

"Hello, watches, bags?"

"Hello, take a picture?"

"Hello, teahouse?"

An elderly homeless woman poked your tits with the lip of a paper cup. The beggar lady shook her cup at your face and the spare change rattled.

Rattling in the skull like coins in an empty cup. Too busy, too much—"Hello, watches, bags, hello, take a picture, hello, teahouse?"—*noise. I envy the static peace those settlers will find on Mars.*

Taxi!

Anywhere but here.

Gridlock.

The driver dug the heel of his palm into the center of the steering wheel. The horn blared, and you stabbed the vinyl seats with the nice pen Mom had given you that time you came home for Christmas.

Mom had wanted you to write home more.

The pen snapped and sprayed ink across the cab. The driver shouted and pulled over. You stretched the holes you had made, shoving fingers into the fabric, tearing and peeling until you could fit your fists into the open seats. You punched down again and again, cutting your knuckles on metal springs. The ink stung the new wounds.

The driver exited, walked around the car, and opened the

rear passenger door. He tried to pull you out. But you held on. With your hands stained red and black, you held on like you'd never been able to before.

And then you caught a glimpse of a woman in the rearview mirror who looked like you.

That is me. I am her. Geri and Deoiridh. Twin pilgrims.

We smile knowingly as the driver barks.

Noise. Never stops.

Never stops barking.

Shut up, or we'll make you.

E-MINUS 00 SECONDS

Livy comes down the stairs. Again, she remarks how the first floor of the house smells like something rotten. Her voice is frantic.

An exploration rover watches Xiumei Dong, the first settler, step out onto the surface of Mars, half a kilometer from the New Plymouth crater.

Xiumei was chosen from thousands of open applicants.

She's a microbiologist and former ESL teacher.

I was a foreign language teacher too.

We squint harder. We touch our nose to the screen, scanning the blurry pixels for any resemblance we might share with Xiumei. We blink and our eyes sting from the light.

I imagine myself as an astronaut falling to Earth in only a spacesuit.

Time is perspective.

The world spins fast, 1,675 kilometers an hour, 465 meters a second, but from above I don't miss a moment.

I finally see everything.

I can see the Himalayas melting. I can trace the layers of erosion with my fingers and follow the runoff of mountain sediment as it falls into the Bay of Bengal. Burning in the troposphere, the heat shatters my sun visor and the sounds of the Earth slam into my ears. The infinite quiet disappears, swallowed by the whoosh and howl of wind and the crackling of my scorched suit. I feel the flames sear an outline of the Indian Ocean onto my retinas.

Livy follows the stench back to the dirty pots in the sink.

She doesn't scream when she discovers that the smell

has originated from more than rancid stew. We barely hear her muffled sobs as she pulls Pocky from beneath the kitchen sink—caked in his own shit, piss, and vomit, stuffed into a pillowcase with his snout and tiny paws bound with shoe stings. Pocky doesn't have enough strength to even whimper.

Livy has nothing left to say.

Perhaps she will finally feel free to leave us in silence.

Because now we know all we've ever wanted was to be alone and remembered.

We've always ached for the world to stop to notice our distance.

And I'm still falling, farther down, singed and grey, faster and faster until my bones shatter against the sea and my skin rips apart, and even then I continue descending, farther down, down into the dim shapeless blue, and then black, down farther still, meters, miles: first through twilight, and then crust, and midnight, mantle, and abyss. I descend, compressed and twisted, through basin and trenches, and slip past unfathomable darkness into core, falling until I might finally rest, consumed by hot, burning light.

OURS

TESTAMENTS

Aarya drags two fingers across the left side of her jaw, lingering over the small scar at the corner of her chin. She begins to hum "Amazing Grace," feigning indifference to Shiloh's questioning. Whenever Aarya feels confronted or attacked, she retreats into gospels.

Shiloh repeats herself. "Don't you think it's weird, Mom?"

Shiloh glances out of the passenger-side window. She has never traveled this far west. Kansas is forever; the flatness stretches for miles on an eternal horizon. Shiloh looks down at the map open on her lap. Aarya opposed purchasing a GPS for the journey and distrusts most electronic advancements since the 1980s, perceiving the tech revolution to be a means by which the devil might conquer more souls. Shiloh traces the progress of their drive along the map with her pinky. Seven hours have passed, and they've barely driven the length of her thumb. They have stopped twice, once for a quick lunch and then a second time to pee.

They haven't spoken since Wichita, when Shiloh threatened to jump from the moving car if she had to listen to another minute of The Prophet and his end-of-days forecast. Aarya reluctantly acquiesced and turned the dial to a different Christian radio station. However, soon after, Aarya began to find many of the commercials too tasteless and offensive. They both agreed to silence then, a quiet truce Shiloh now threatened to break.

"Mom, you can at least recognize that the date and time are odd? How and why did God decide to end the world on the twenty-first of May? Is there any Biblical significance?"

Aarya prides herself on her patience. Shiloh is refractory and caustic. Often Aarya doubts whether she likes her own daughter. She asks herself if attempts to save Shiloh truly come from motherly devotion or a sense of duty to lead impenitent sinners to salvation.

"The world is not ending, Shiloh," Aarya says. "It is the beginning of the rapture. The physical world will not be destroyed, not yet, just cleansed. And if it were another date, would it seem less specific? If the rapture were on the third of December, would it be easier for you to believe?"

Shiloh considers her mother's rebuttal, surprised by how

well Aarya employs reasonable arguments to an illogical premise. Her mom's Urdu-tinged English accent lends authority to her statements. Aarya has the cadence of an Oxford-educated Pakistani prime minister—a Christian Benazir Bhutto.

"No, I suppose not," Shiloh says. "But then I guess I have difficulty accepting the idea of the whole of civilization, with the exception of this special select group, being annihilated by fires, earthquakes, and plagues."

Aarya begins to sing openly, her hands squeezing the wheel. *Amazing Grace, how sweet the sound, that saved a wretch like me.* She repeats the chorus twice before addressing Shiloh again.

"You have difficulty with fires, earthquakes, and plagues? These are things you can feel and see, proof of God's might."

"Or nature."

Aarya often prays that Shiloh's refusal of the Holy Spirit is only a test. Aarya prays that the efforts to redeem her daughter are one day rewarded. Aarya will rest better believing that, when she meets God for judgment, she did all she could to save Shiloh. Aarya returns to singing, louder now. *I once was lost, but now am found. Was blind, but now I see!*

"You know that song was written by a slave trader, right?"

"Exactly."

They both fall silent, at ease for the moment.

~~~

When people ask Shiloh Najjar about her name, she explains its religious context. She tells them, "It means a gift from God, or something like that." Aarya had named Shiloh. Shiloh's father had no input, having disappeared long before the time came to name her. Shiloh had only met her father once. She had just turned seven. His name was Johnathan Rekdall, and Aarya admitted to having married him to gain American citizenship. He was a trucker, bald and skinny except for his large belly drooping over his belt, pregnant with beer. Shiloh remembers his hands most of all, his crooked fingers curved like hooks. When he pinched Shiloh's cheeks, his rough digits had scratched her face.

Johnathan appeared one morning at Aarya's apartment to apologize for abandoning them. He said he had found Jesus and he wanted to be a better man. He wanted a fresh start and to do the right thing by his daughter. They all spent one perfect day together: shopping, dinner, and a movie—Shiloh's only theatrical experience until the tenth grade when she defied her mother's forbiddance and began sneaking to movie matinees after school with some of the money she earned from babysitting. When Shiloh and her father returned home after nightfall, Shiloh refused to sleep, fearing that if she closed her eyes, her dad would vanish. He carried her to bed, tucked her in the way she had always imagined he would, and then he kissed her forehead goodnight. That was the last night Shiloh had really prayed for anything, for her father to stay. The next morning he was gone.

While weeping into her mother's lap the following morning, Shiloh did not realize that in her father's absence she would become the sole witness to her mother's religious fanaticism. Shiloh would bear the burden of having to watch Aarya delve deeper into extremism, inevitably condemning and alienating everyone. By the time Shiloh reached high school, she had developed a deep cynicism and contempt for religion.

But she managed to abide her mother's loud, insistent prayers five times a day: a prayer when she woke up, when she went to bed, and before every meal. Shiloh learned to forgive her mother for occasionally mailing in their grocery money to televangelist ministries. Shiloh taught herself to pardon Aarya for attending book burnings and anti-gay rallies. She tolerated the cheesy blue-eyed, blonde-haired iconography on every wall of their house—their great white savior staring down on Shiloh every time she used the bathroom. Shiloh tried to exercise patience whenever Aarya proselytized to strangers or the friends Shiloh made the mistake of bringing home from school. Shiloh endured these things, knowing that one day soon she would leave for college. She had worked and saved, and soon she'd be free from the weight of her mother's Christian guilt.

And so, when Aarya came storming into Shiloh's room, shouting about how some blessed messenger had calculated when the world would finally end, Shiloh agreed to leave with her mother after some minor protest. Shiloh made a conscious effort to keep her opinion to her herself as they loaded their Ford Taurus and started the long journey west to California to join the believers gathering in Oakland. A part of Shiloh even welcomed the trip. The journey would be poetic, Shiloh thought. Aarya driving toward the end of the world while Shiloh saw her own life about to really begin.

She'd accompany her mom and she wouldn't fuss about it, not as much she usually did. And when time finally revealed her mother's lapse in judgment, Shiloh would be there to comfort Aarya, or to rub the truth in her face.

~~~

They stop for the night at a roadside motel just over the border of Utah. The location reminds Shiloh of a relic from some Hitchcock-era thriller. Accented by blood-red carpet, curtains, and linens, Shiloh suggests their cash-only room would suit an affair or a murder. Aarya doesn't find the joke funny.

Everything smells like smoke. There is one queen-sized bed. Exhausted, Aarya doesn't have the energy to complain. She reminds Shiloh that this is the best they can afford. Shiloh nods in quiet concession, understanding that her mother's income as a medical receptionist does not allow for luxury. Shiloh wonders briefly how her mother has financed their journey. She imagines her mother is accruing even more debt for this spiritual jaunt.

Aarya lets her daughter shower first. Although she has done the majority of the driving, miles and miles of pumping brakes and steering through the Rockies, Aarya's legs are still restless. She retrieves their luggage from the backseat of the car. She and

Shiloh share a single suitcase, heavy but manageable. There is a lesson, Aarya thinks, in reducing a lifetime of worldly possessions into one bag. There are essentials, but not really. She contemplates the Hebrews leaving Egypt. What little they had, He had made enough. God will do the same for her. He is all she needs. This is her exodus.

Shiloh calls from behind the bathroom door. "Mom, can you pass me a towel, please? I forgot to bring one in here with me." Aarya rummages through the suitcase and pulls out a towel. She walks over to the bathroom door and then knocks. Shiloh's hand pokes out from behind door. "I don't know why I would assume that this place would have one." Shiloh snatches the towel. "Thanks." The door slams shut again.

"Make sure to hang it up once you're done. It's our only one, okay?"

Shiloh doesn't reply.

Aarya decides to fetch ice for the room. They have no cups or glasses, but there is a bucket on the dresser. She remembers seeing a rust-spotted metal ice machine in the lobby next to the service desk. Aarya announces to Shiloh that she will be back shortly and then exits the room.

Aarya crosses the parking lot, a giant asphalt C around a swimming pool with brackish water. There aren't many cars, five excluding her own. The vicinity is quiet. Silhouettes against the window curtains and the flicker from television screens are the only proof of life. She thinks about the other inhabitants of the motel on pilgrimages of their own. She thinks of their sins and the decisions that brought her and them to occupy the same place. She prays for them silently, that they should get their lives in order for God's reckoning.

Pulling open the single glass door, she slides inside the lobby. At the front desk is the elderly East-Indian man who checked her in earlier. He is listening to a woman talk about tornadoes in the Midwest on a digital radio cupped in his hands. The clock floating on the wall behind him is at eleven and twelve.

"Good evening, again," Aarya says.

The motel attendant smiles broadly, revealing rows of straight teeth stained by coffee.

"Good evening," he replies.

His voice carries a sincerity that sounds like more than just customer service. He is an old acquaintance, not a close friend, but someone with whom there exists an intimate knowledge of a place most people have never seen. The man reminds Aarya of her father.

She hasn't seen her parents since the day she left Bradford. She tried to explain it to them, the truth she had found in Jesus Christ, and how Freddy had taught her to pray. They didn't see the same thing. They condemned her, calling her vile and used. They shunned her and she became a stranger to them. But their distance made her grow stronger in her faith. She had to accept the fact that some people, most people, cannot truly be saved. She left as soon as she was old enough, and like Lot fleeing from Sodom, she never looked back.

"May I help you?"

"Oh, yes. I'm sorry. Ice, please." Aarya raises her bucket.

The man nods, sets down the radio, and shuffles around the front desk to the large ice chest by the lobby entrance. He moves carefully as if trying not to disrupt the stillness of the room. He unlocks the padlock and raises the large, flat door to the bin. Aarya doesn't understand the need for a lock. She notices a sign on the counter that reads FREE ICE. She wonders what could have happened to encourage these measures, and it makes her anxious. In what type of place—in what kind of world—can people not be trusted with free frozen water?

Without speaking the old man instructs her to scoop out the ice. She fills her bucket and thanks him. He closes the bin and replaces the padlock.

Aarya feels sorry for him. He seems like a nice man, undeserving of spending his last days on Earth looking after ice in a dirty motel.

"You know, God's time is almost among us? Repent, accept His Son into your heart, and you may be granted eternal life."

The motel attendant stares back at her incredulously.

"Do you mind me asking where are you coming from?" he asks.

"I'm from Missouri. My daughter and I are heading west to join other believers in Oakland."

The motel attendant flashes a knowing grin. "Ah, I heard about people like you on the radio," he says, pointing to the talking black box on the counter. "You are heading west to see Carol Hamlin?"

"The Prophet Carol Hamlin, yes."

The old man's face grows somber. He shuffles behind the counter.

"That man is not a prophet. The world is not going to end the day after tomorrow."

"But Prophet Hamlin is a holy, smart man. Using numerology, he has..."

"No one man can know the day or hour these things will happen, not even the angels in heaven or the Son himself." The man points to the ceiling, never taking his eyes off Aarya. "Only the Father knows. Matthew said that."

"Matthew?"

"The book of Matthew. I am Catholic."

Aarya looks down at the bucket of ice. She would like to tell the man that believing in Christ isn't enough. She had practiced several different denominations—Jehovah's Witness to Methodist to Catholic to Baptist to Calvinist to Mormon, back to Jehovah's Witness, and so on—but when she finally heard Carol Hamlin as she was flipping through cable channels late one night in the nurses' break room, she knew she had finally found the truth. His message was not about affiliation or finding redemption; it was about destruction, the end. And it spoke to some deep-seated belief she had always held: the world yearns for destruction. She thanks the man, choosing to avoid conflict, and heads back to her room.

~~~

Aarya's journey to Prophet Hamlin had started many years earlier, on a not unusually dreary afternoon in Bradford, West Yorkshire—both the whites and the Kashmiris often called the town Bradistan. While at home alone that day, Aarya heard a knock at the front door, too timid for a relative or a postal worker. She opened the door to find one of her schoolmates, an upperclassman. She knew his name, Freddy, a stern boy with buzzed strawberry blond hair.

"Hello," he said, staring, expectant.

Aarya had never seen Freddy look unkempt. He was particularly clean that day, dressed in a spotless white button-down Oxford and pressed black slacks, clutching a book to his abdomen. The title read *Reasoning from the Scriptures*. At school Aarya tried not to notice Freddy, his brilliant green eyes, his barrel chest strong and round like a storybook prince. Sometimes on her way to work at her mother's saree shop, Aarya would go by the park to catch a glimpse of Freddy, shirtless, kicking a ball around with other kids whose families could afford for them not to have a part-time job. Sometimes Aarya would tuck herself behind a tree and watch him move.

"Eh, what's your name?"

"Aarya Najjar," she replied, a little disappointed but not all that surprised that Freddy didn't know her name. At school they fell on opposing ends of the social spectrum—Freddy popular, coveted, and Aarya commonly known as *the Paki with the tits*.

"I'm glad you were home, Aarya. My friends and I are making our weekly visit to the neighborhood to share the wonderful things that God's Kingdom will do for mankind." He furrowed his brow, and for a moment Aarya caught a glimpse of what he might look like as an older man. Still distinguished, she thought, and handsome. Her stomach stirred and her face felt hot.

"That's a pretty name, Aarya."

"Thank you."

"Aarya, do you know Jesus Christ?"

"He's a prophet, right?"

Freddy laughed. "Yes, but he was so much more than that. Can I share a message with you?" She nodded and he began leafing through his book. He stopped on a page and placed his finger on a line of text. "The book of Revelation says, 'Look! God's dwelling place is now among the people, and he will dwell with them. They will be his people, and God himself will be with them and be their God. He will wipe every tear from their eyes. There will be no more death or mourning or crying or pain, for the old order of things has passed away.'" Freddy closed the book and returned her gaze. "What do you think about that, Aarya? Does it sound good to you?"

She noticed his jaw, brawny and accented by a crooked little blemish in the shape of a V at the left corner of his chin. She had once overheard Freddy tell a friend about how the scar came from a dive during a game of cricket. Whenever Aarya thought about Freddy's jaw, she imagined how it would feel nuzzled under her chin, tightening and loosening and tightening as his lips pursed against her neck and his tongue slid down to her collarbone. Then she would feel wetness between her legs and she'd have to pinch the inside of her thighs to make it stop. She didn't know where these thoughts originated, and she feared them. If any of her friends had also been thinking about touching boys, they never mentioned these feelings to Aarya. They had crushes—on Trevor Horn from The Buggles mostly—but none of them ever said anything about having *urges*. Aarya had no proof, but she had determined that these emotions had coincided with the development of her breasts. They had grown quickly and she seemed to rise from bed one morning with two cantaloupes on her chest. When none of her turtlenecks fit anymore, Aarya tried wearing her mother's abaya to school. She noticed some of the boys became nicer. Some girls became friendlier too. She was surprised that even in her mother's long, black, shapeless frock her new body could warrant so much attention.

She had never received that kind of attention from Freddy. He looked through her, if at all. Even at that moment, he stood in her doorway, looking inside and past her.

"I don't know," Aarya said.

"Sure you do," Freddy replied.

"It sounds nice, I guess." She had in fact really liked the sound of it, a world with no pain or death, but Freddy had been standing there too long. It didn't look right, an older white boy in this neighborhood chatting to her. If Freddy stood outside much longer, a neighbor would see him and then they'd tell her parents once they came home from the silk mill.

"Look, my family is Muslim; we pray to Allah."

Freddy smiled again. "Eh, and what about you?"

"What do you mean?"

"You said your *family* is Muslim. What do you believe, Aarya?"

"I don't know. But I really need to go."

"No, I think you do know. I think you know that Allah can't save you."

Aarya stood, shocked silent by his rudeness. She considered what to do. Her father would slam the door in Freddy's face. Her mother would threaten to call the police. Aarya should find Freddy's behavior inexcusable. She should feel offended.

Freddy spoke with the same playful self-assurance he displayed during athletics. Aarya wanted to know that confidence. She wanted to know whatever made him so righteous.

"Save me from what?" Aarya asked.

"The end of the world," he said, smiling again. "These are the last days, Aarya. Wouldn't you like the absolute assurance of salvation?"

Freddy didn't wait for an answer. He turned and walked away.

~~~

Aarya enters the motel room. Her mind wanders like it does before shutting down for sleep each night, skipping from point to point, reviewing the day and making predictions for tomorrow.

Shiloh sits at the corner of the bed, legs folded in a pair of pajama pants, reading over a stack of college brochures. Below her, the damp used towel lies crumpled on the floor. She has pulled her wet hair up into a bun and tiny trails of water drip down the back of her neck, soaking parts of her large T-shirt. On the tee, beneath a reversed Nike swoosh, are the words *Just Do It: Live For Jesus* with a cross replacing the T in *It*. It is one of a dozen religious shirts gifted to Shiloh that she refuses to wear in public. Aarya has a tendency toward clothes that are modest and loose fitting. But at seventeen years old, Shiloh seems to have cultivated a sense of style that complements her ample body. Shiloh is beautiful, blessed, Aarya thinks. Shiloh has her father's olive green eyes and her mother's rope-thick hair and eyebrows. Sometimes Aarya hurts looking at Shiloh, thinking about how painful it might be to watch her daughter, a stunning young woman, die.

"Why are you staring at me?" Shiloh asks without looking up from her pamphlets.

Aarya walks to the dresser and sets down the bucket. "I went to get ice."

"Do we have any cups?"

"No, but just in case."

"Just in case of what?"

"It's here if you need it, Shiloh, okay?" Aarya moves to the edge of the bed, stoops to pick up the towel, and then heads to the bathroom. She hangs the towel on a green-stained rod and then returns to her daughter. Aarya sits next to Shiloh on the bed.

"What are you reading?"

"Right now, it is the summer orientation welcome packet from Missouri Southern State University. It's next weekend. They're saying I can go ahead and register online for fall classes. When I applied, I said I wanted to go into media journalism, but now I'm thinking film."

"Next weekend?" Aarya rises. She shuffles to an alcove where she has left the suitcase. She kneels over her luggage and then unzips the bag. She searches the contents for clothes to wear to sleep.

Shiloh continues. "I thought we could also look at schools in the Bay Area. I figured if we are already there, why not? I might want to try to transfer one day."

Aarya's hands pause. Her eyes dart over the objects in bag, but she cannot see past her growing fury. "Shiloh, there won't be a next weekend."

Shiloh raises her head. "Next weekend, I'm borrowing the car and driving to the MSSU campus."

"Oh, Shiloh."

Shiloh bounces to her feet. "Don't patronize me. I've tried to be patient with you, I really have. You're delusional."

Aarya slams the suitcase closed. "Being a Christian does not make me delusional."

"Being a Christian has nothing to do with how you are acting, Mom. There are literally millions of Christians all over the globe who aren't like you, who aren't following the ramblings of this crazy old man. Do you realize he has predicted Armageddon before, twice? He was wrong then. What makes you think he's got it right this time?"

"Because I know."

"How do you know?"

"I just do. I have faith."

"In this man?"

"In God. I have faith in God, in his judgment. The world is corrupt and wicked, and there are people who walk around thinking they are free of punishment. They do terrible things and they think they get away with it, but they can't. There is an order. I have faith that God will punish them."

Shiloh chuckles to herself, folds her arms, and widens her stance, settling in for a long fight. "You believe in heaven because there has to be a hell?"

"I believe that we all will have to face a power greater than our own. We can't save ourselves."

"Mom, have you ever heard the story about the Christian man and the flood?"

"Noah?"

"No."

Aarya sits on the bed and folds her arms.

"Okay, in a small remote town there was this really bad storm, and local officials sent out an emergency warning that the river would overflow. They ordered people to evacuate, but this one Christian man heard the warning and decided to stay. He expected God to save him, to greet him with some heavenly miracle. So he just sat there. The neighbors came by his house and tried to offer him a seat in their car, but the man said no. He wouldn't move. 'God will save me,' he said. The man waited. The water rose up the steps of his porch, up to his front door. Another man in a canoe paddled by and saw him. He offered to take the Christian man to safety, but of course he shot him down, saying, 'God will save me.' The floodwaters rose higher and higher until he was forced to climb onto his roof. A helicopter spotted him and sent down a rope ladder. A rescue officer came down and told him to take his hand and he would pull him up. And do you know what the man did?"

Aarya glares at Shiloh. "He refused."

"Yes, of course! He sat on his hands and said, 'No, thank you. God will save me.' Well, the guy drowned after suffering from dehydration and starvation. When he made it to the gates of heaven, the man stood before God and asked why, after putting all of his faith in God, had he not come to save him. And God laughed at him and said, 'I sent you a warning. I sent you a car. I sent you a canoe. I sent you a helicopter.'"

Aarya gently rubs the left side of her jaw. "Okay, and?"

"If there is a God—*if*—wouldn't it be more likely that she would be the type to help those who believe in helping themselves? Wouldn't God have greater admiration for the folks who try to save themselves, people who try to make the most of it here on Earth instead of waiting unreasonably for an afterlife?"

"Faith doesn't have to be unreasonable. God can work through others, yes. And I believe He is working through Carol Hamlin. I don't pretend to understand God's plan, but I have never heard His voice so clearly. He wants us to go to Oakland."

Shiloh flings her arms up in defeat and collapses onto the bed.

"Whatever, Mom."

Shaking her head, Shiloh returns to scanning over her college information packets. Aarya frowns and continues her absent-minded search for something to wear to bed. She picks a long nightgown and retreats to the bathroom. When Aarya exits after changing clothes and brushing her teeth, the motel room is dark and Shiloh has nestled in bed under the blankets. Aarya peels back the covers and slides onto the mattress. She uses care to avoid disturbing Shiloh, although Aarya suspects Shiloh is only pretending to sleep.

After minutes of staring into the darkness, they both fall into a cautious sleep, shallow like their breathing, always mindful of the space between them.

~~~

After the twelfth time her mother tried to find a sign from God in a passing license plate—GWA84U (*God Waits for You*), D3ND21 (*The End, 21st*), KGSAA (*Keep Going, Shiloh and Aarya*)—Shiloh offered to drive while Aarya slept. Shiloh has driven through most of Nevada and California, and has nearly passed Daly City on I-280. While her mom rests, Shiloh decides to drive around the bay to get a glimpse of San Francisco—a city she has developed an affinity for through films.

She veers right off Interstate 80 toward the Bay Bridge, heading east to Oakland. A fog has rolled in off the Pacific and settled around the city. The tops of buildings poke through the clouds like the spines of a giant puffer fish. As she crosses over the bridge and into downtown Oakland, Shiloh envisions herself as a denizen of the city on a morning commute.

Even though no proven correlation exists between one's success in life and their ability to read a map, Shiloh is impressed with herself for not having to wake her mother to navigate. She likes to consider this a sign that she will do well when the time comes to leave her mother.

Shiloh recognizes their destination immediately. Hundreds of believers are gathered, blocking all but one lane of eastbound traffic in front of Carol Hamlin's radio headquarters—an unassuming two-story building with a pointed roof and an all-glass front, tucked between a psychic and an auto body shop. Shiloh finds street parking several blocks away before waking her mother. Aarya rises slowly in her seat. Her eyes flutter open to peer through the passenger-side window.

Shiloh watches her mother. In the side-view mirror, she sees fear in Aarya's expression. Minutes pass and Aarya makes no effort to exit the car. Shiloh studies the back of Aarya's head as it slides from right to left, tailing passing families with Bibles and signs until they disappear at the end of the block. Aarya's hands tremble in her lap.

It is one thing to talk about the end of man, and it's another thing to believe it, Shiloh thinks.

Aarya tucks her fingers into fists and slides them between her thighs. A sympathetic quiver rushes down Shiloh's spine, and her heart pounds in her ears.

"Mom, we don't have to go out there," Shiloh says. "I should have never let you come here."

Aarya pats Shiloh's knee.

They sit a while longer, watching the crowds march toward the end.

~~~

Aarya recalls having to sneak a copy of the *New World Translation of the Holy Scriptures* into her house. Her parents considered themselves progressive. However, Aarya often overheard them sympathize with Iran's Ayatollah Khomeini, especially his belief that everyday political and social issues should be interpreted through the filter of the Islamic faith. Despite fears of her parents finding out about her weekly scripture study with Freddy,

Aarya continued to convene with him every Tuesday in her family's dining room while no one else was home.

At school, Freddy continued to ignore her, failing to acknowledge any familiarity even when they literally ran into each other. Aarya often walked with her head down to avoid eye contact and once, coming around a corner, she had collided with Freddy, dropping her books and thoroughly embarrassing herself. While Freddy's friends berated Aarya—*You're a clumsy one aren't ya, Tits?* and *Ay, Tits, how about next time you ram those zeppelins into me?*—Freddy stared at her blankly. Eventually, he bent down to help collect her stuff from the floor with the polite formality of a kind stranger.

Aarya never brought this up during their lessons, fearful that she would upset him and he would vanish. She had begun to relate to what Freddy taught her.

"All Christian denominations are demonic in origin," Freddy had said. "Catholics, Protestants, Lutherans, Episcopalians—their gospels are false and they have all abandoned the true faith. The New Testament even confirms it. It says a mass falling away will occur before the end times."

"End times?"

"Yeah, Aarya. The end of the world. It's coming, sure as the air we breathe."

Finally, Aarya had an explanation for all of the anxiety and dread she carried. A part of her must have always known the world would soon come to an end.

"Does your dad work for a mill?"

"Yes."

"What if the mill were to close? What would he do?"

"I guess he could go to another mill."

"And what if that one closed?"

"Try another. There a plenty of mills in Bradford."

"But with computers, who is to say we will even need guys like your father in the future? They could probably just build a robot to do what your father does. It would never get tired or need a day off and you and your family would be homeless and poor."

"That can't really happen, right?"

"It could. The cost of living is getting higher and innovation is making jobs obsolete. Crime, illness, and death are on the rise. Do you think it's reasonable to expect that our government can really solve all these problems? Aarya, do you feel there is any solution to these things here on Earth?"

"No, I suppose there isn't."

"It's right there in Ezekiel 9, everyone is being marked, either for preservation through the great tribulation or for destruction by God. We can't save ourselves."

Freddy had answers to questions Aarya had never asked herself. She found that more and more, she wanted to agree with him.

And then one day Freddy told her that only 144,000 would earn anointment as judges at Jesus' side. The rest would die and cease to exist or receive resurrection on Earth for all eternity.

"But there are so few destined for heaven, how can anything I do ever be enough?"

"Your grace is enough, Aarya. All he requires of you is to love, to surrender yourself."

Freddy leaned across the table and kissed her. Stunned, Aarya yanked her head back, but he gripped her neck and pulled her forward, ramming his tongue deep into her mouth.

"Wait," she grunted, pushing him back with her arms. "What are you doing?"

"To love is one of God's commandments, Aarya. Do you love me?"

"I don't know."

He kissed her neck, and there was his perfect jaw nestled under her chin, but not as she had imagined. And then her face was down on the dining room floor, Freddy suddenly on top of her with his damp palm pinning her head to the carpet. She felt his other hand streak across her body, tearing and pulling at her clothes. He pushed, over and over again. A tree scorched by lightning, ripped in a violent wind, doused in the roar of rain so heavy Aarya couldn't hear herself plead, "Stop. Please. Not like this."

Freddy apologized when he finished, but not to her. He returned to his knees and began to repent. He left crying.

He never returned to the house.

He continued to overlook Aarya at school.

But Freddy had left his mark, a large rug burn on the left side of Aarya's jaw that would never fully heal.

~~~

Rubbing the scar beside her chin, Aarya exits the car. Shiloh follows her mother and the pair trails a group carrying megaphones and papier-mâché crosses. Shiloh and Aarya push through rows of police officers, spectators, and news anchors before reaching Hamlin's believers. Dozens of disciples sit cross-legged in prayer circles, nodding in agreement with roaming pastors. The ministers shout of fire and brimstone and slap Bibles for emphasis. Curious, Shiloh wades deeper into the mass of bodies, and Aarya moves behind her. They are swallowed into the standing crowds.

Among the believers there are different demonstrations of faith. Most gaze up at the radio tower stationed at the tip of the roof. The steel spire reaches for heaven like a steeple. Many have their eyes closed and their heads bowed, listening attentively to Carol Hamlin as he address the congregation through a pair of civil defense sirens posted at the front corners of the building.

"The time is here, my brothers and sisters," The Prophet says. "We, the true believers, will receive the reward for our faith. We will be raptured. God knows who His elect are!"

Many cheer, raising their heads, stretching their arms out to the sky, ready to receive God's reckoning.

Beneath Hamlin's steady stream of consciousness, Shiloh imagines hearing Aarya's heavy breathing. Shiloh turns to her mother. Aarya's legs shake visibly. Shiloh, several inches taller, wraps an arm around her mother's waist to keep her from falling.

The Prophet announces that the hour has come—3 p.m., Pacific Standard Time.

The volume of the crowd grows louder, and the hum of whispered prayers matches the volume of Hamlin's rambling.

Aarya throws her arms around Shiloh and sobs into her hair.

"I'm sorry," she says. "I know it couldn't have been easy for you. I can be difficult, and if you ever felt as if I was forcing my opinions on you, it was only because I was trying to protect you."

"I know, Mom." Shiloh says. "I'm sorry too."

At 3:59, a silent countdown begins among the believers.

Hamlin is the only voice as he screams of eternal life in the kingdom of heaven.

Shiloh begins to question: What if she is wrong and the universe is far stranger than she thought possible? For the first time since her father left, Shiloh joins her mother in quiet, earnest prayer. She hears her mother pray for cleansing fire, for merciful justice against the wicked who prey on the weak. Her mother pleads for the Lord to strike against the corrupted Earth.

But Shiloh prays for the survival of humanity.

She begs God to reconsider.

When Shiloh opens her eyes again, it is 4:01.

People gathered beyond the crowd of believers laugh.

Shiloh turns to her mother. Aarya stares at Carol Hamlin's headquarters, still waiting. A plastic bottle flies past Shiloh's head and crashes at her feet. Another bottle sails above, followed by several others. Shiloh hears heavy objects smashing through glass. She stands on the tips of her toes to catch a glimpse of a brick shattering a large windowpane at the front of the radio station.

Shiloh grabs her mother's wrists. "Mom, we need to go."

Turning around, Shiloh tries to push through waves of people crashing toward Hamlin's headquarters.

"Wait," Aarya shouts. "He hasn't given an explanation. He hasn't told us what to do next."

Shiloh tugs her mother. "There isn't an explanation."

"No."

"He was a fake, Mom." She pulls harder, guiding Aarya through the swarming believers.

"No. No, this can't be. There must be a reason. Something must have happened. God told me. There must be a reason."

Shiloh presses against the gauntlet of limbs and torsos, dragging her mother through the crowd.

"Excuse me, ma'am...There is no reason, Mom...Excuse me. Pardon me...He was a just a crazy old man."

"But I quit my job. I stopped paying rent. Oh, Shiloh."

"You quit your job?" Shiloh pauses to check her mother's face. "You stopped paying rent on our apartment? Why? Why would you do that?"

"Shiloh, I thought..."

"No. What else?"

Aarya's eyes cloud with new tears.

"Your money, Shiloh...I borrowed your check card. I couldn't pay for this trip by myself. I just didn't have enough in the bank."

"My money? The money I've been saving for college?"

"I did it to save you, Shiloh. I had to bring you here. God told me to bring you here."

"To save me? You are not a savior, Mom. You are not one of the Bible's great heroes. You are a sad, delusional woman."

"There is nothing delusional about having faith."

"This isn't what faith is."

Shiloh drops her mother's hand and pushes back to the car, alone.

Aarya rises onto the balls of her feet to take a final look at The Prophet's headquarters as believers rush through the broken office windows.

~~~

They set out early the next day for the long ride home to Missouri. Shiloh does the majority of the driving. She chooses the radio stations and sings along to secular tunes as loudly as she can, even the Top 40 hits that she can't stand, daring her mother to say anything.

Aarya's silence echoes the desert roads of Nevada, quiet miles of dirt and nothing. Aarya asks to stop only once, for food.

Shiloh finds a small diner. The server asks them what they want to drink and if they would like her to turn on the TV.

"We've got satellite," she says, pointing to an old tube set mounted near the ceiling in one corner of the dining area.

Shiloh asks to watch a headline news station. The server flips between channels, past flashes of daytime soap operas, game shows, and golf tournaments until the television fades in on images of destruction. Shiloh gasps at clouds of smoke rolling out of random fires; piles of debris; splintered trees; and overturned cars, trucks, and trailers.

Aarya recognizes the landscape immediately, the remnants of their home in Missouri.

At the bottom of the screen, the scrolling feed reads "Deadly Tornado." Newscasters say an EF5 multiple-vortex tornado one mile in width has raked across the city, injuring hundreds and killing 162.

Shiloh considers the event a terrible catastrophe.

Aarya sees a reward for her conviction.

Shiloh will explain the science of tornadoes, how cold air from the Rockies and Canada collide with warm air from the Gulf of Mexico, and how an F3 hit the city in May of 1971.

Aarya will explain how following her faith saved their lives.

Shiloh will use the words *natural disaster* and *coincidence*.

Aarya will speak of *Acts of God* and *Divine Will*.

The truth may always stand between them.

A SELFISH INVENTION

Into a dingy embankment of snow lining the cracked sidewalk to her residence hall, DaYana drops the butt of her cigarette. She exhales a final exasperated cloud of wet, grey smoke and watches the vapors scatter in the frigid air. Glancing down at the beige stub steaming on the packed ice, DaYana considers the contribution she has made to the billion pounds of non-biodegradable cigarette ends that become toxic trash each year. DaYana folds her arms and shivers against a sudden chill slipping under her hooded peacoat and over her shaved head. She curses herself for breaking her promise to quit smoking, and then curses herself for choosing to attend graduate school in New England. Shuffling quickly up the steps to the front lobby of her dorm, she chides herself for not being asleep and for coming out into the cold and for fretting over negative workshop feedback.

DaYana pulls open one of the heavy steel commercial doors. She stomps her feet on the large entrance mats, but the squeak of her damp boots still echoes against the rubber tiles of the stairwell. Climbing to the third level, she decides to abandon the revisions she's made over the last few hours. She forms a plan: She will use the bathroom and then head to her room to go to bed. She'll snooze through the morning craft lectures and awake in the afternoon with fresh eyes and hopefully a better perspective on her piece and the "cultural incongruities" which her workshop leader and cohorts claim make the story feel less capital-A-authentic.

She arrives at her floor and pauses in the doorway. Darkness shrouds the halls—part of the college's initiative to conserve energy. The only light emanates from the glowing red emergency exit sign mounted above her.

"Authentic," DaYana says aloud to no one, letting the word linger in the quiet shadows as she slinks through the black toward the direction of the communal lavatories.

Pushing through the swinging bathroom door, DaYana squints against the harsh fluorescence. She recites silently the opening lines of her story.

The hardships and joys of labor make a solid symphony. Leo knew this. If you hear one of the others tell you they predicted Leo's betrayal, do not listen. In truth, Leo worked hard and the company rewarded him. He started at seventeen in raw materials plant 6/20. He moved on to the assembly line in factory five. By twenty-five, he had become a tester on the third shift, a very comfortable...

DaYana nearly stumbles as the tip of one of her insulated steel-toed snow boots hits a body curled on the restroom floor.

DaYana hops over the figure. Her drowsy brain struggles to process the scene. She stands for several seconds scanning the mass before squatting down to examine. DaYana reaches out a hand and shakes the snoring carcass. The body wakes, coughing and sputtering.

"Phillip Dawkins?" DaYana hears herself say.

The distinguished visiting faculty nods. "You're a woman?"

"Yes," DaYana says.

"What are you doing in the men's room?"

"All the bathrooms in this dorm are gender neutral."

Phillip Dawkins blinks slowly. "Jesus Christ."

DaYana can hear the audible clicks and creaks from the old man's bones as Dawkins sits up with a groan. He scans the restroom and asks, "Do you know what happened to the young lady who was here a moment ago?"

"No."

"You sure? She was just here. A girl. Her breasts are substantial but not gratuitous, you know? Falling from her chest but not drooping, they tug at her clavicle, creating pockets deep enough to carry sips of water between her collarbones and her long, elegant neck?"

"No. Sorry."

"But you know who I mean, right? She's perfect. She's got a celestial nose, the tip turned up slightly like her face was built to point to the heavens."

DaYana claps her palms together. "Okay. I'm done with this. I got to pee."

She stands and walks to the farthest stall.

After relieving her swollen bladder, she emerges to find Dawkins swaying on his feet and gripping the sides of a sink to balance himself.

DaYana leaves a basin between them as she washes her hands.

"There was a party this evening over in faculty housing," Dawkins explains. "Someone was kind enough to share their barrel-aged gin. As things cooled over there, I thought to cross that frozen tundra of a campus in search of warmer jubilation. That's when I discovered that striking young woman in one of the downstairs common rooms taking shots of champagne, if you can believe it." Dawkins' hacking laugh is a piercing bark against the bathroom's porcelain surfaces. He pauses suddenly to glance across the room again. "Where did she go?"

"I don't know," DaYana says, shaking her hands to dry them.

She moves around Dawkins to exit the room, but he calls after her, "You're Diana, correct?"

"DaYana, like DAY and ANNA." She turns to face him. "I'm in your specialized workshop. You critiqued me earlier today. Well, yesterday."

Dawkins squints and nods. "That's correct. I liked your story's premise. Chinese factory worker dies trying to build a teleportation machine with smuggled parts from a microwave oven assembly line. It's interesting enough."

"Really? Because during workshop you said my piece was 'static, colorful static.' Then I just had to sit there while you asked other students to rewrite my opening and read their alternative versions with you interrupting them every few lines to say, 'Do you see what they did there, Diana?' It was pretty awful."

"Does criticism of your work offend you? If you hope to be a better writer, you'll have to be open to a little feedback."

"Hey, I'm sorry, but that's bullshit. I'm open to constructive criticism. That's not what that was. I mean, you barely said anything about my story beyond the first page, just vague assertions about how some of the cultural aspects of the narrative didn't feel believable."

DaYana pulls back her hood. She runs her cold hands across her buzzed scalp, yawns, and shakes her head. "I'm going to bed. I guess I'll see you tomorrow."

Dawkins wobbles closer. "I apologize if you perceived my guidance as less than thorough. I can tell you exactly how you can improve, Diana. If you aren't too tired, we can even discuss your fiction now, while your prose is still relatively fresh in my mind."

DaYana studies the crystalized drool at the corner of Dawkins' mouth leading to a thin matted line of hair across part of his bushy grey beard. His red, vein-streaked eyes shake rapidly behind his horn-rimmed glasses.

"Okay. Sure."

"Great. Might I trouble you for a cigarette? The nicotine does help me think."

"How do you know I smoke?"

Dawkins narrows his eyes. "You have a gross compulsion to nibble the skin around your fingernails. I've noticed you doing this during workshop. You're even doing it now. This betrays an oral fixation or sexual frustration, and although I'm not entirely prepared to exclude the possibility that you might be starved for intercourse, you're wearing a coat and boots, your face is red, and you obviously just came in from the cold. The only thing that would compel a person to venture out into below freezing temperatures this late at night is vice."

"Fair enough," DaYana says, pulling her fingers away from her mouth. "But if you were able to figure out that I just came inside, why would I go back out there?"

"We won't be long. We'll smoke quickly, imbue our lungs with warm tobacco, and return indoors to talk about your writing."

DaYana senses the tug of sleep behind her pupils, but her extremities surge with excitement.

She relents. "Fine."

Dawkins beams, removing his hands from the edges of the

sink and stumbling to the restroom door.

Peering out into the hallway, Dawkins gasps. "Who vanished the light?" he asks.

DaYana strides next to him. She removes her smartphone from her coat and taps on a flashlight application. The pair move to the stairs.

"Diana, do you think that young woman resides on this floor?"

"We should try to keep our voices down. People are sleeping."

"Should we go in search of her? Should we attempt to wake her?"

"No."

On the stairs, Dawkins' caution surprises DaYana. He turns his body sideways, both hands white knuckled on the railing. Dawkins continues to chat about the girl he met earlier and dubs her his missing muse.

"She reminds me very much of my first wife who was a dancer, trained in classical and interpretive, not a stripper or anything of the sort, although we did meet in a dive bar, HA!"

Again Dawkins expels his explosive biting laugh, filling the stairwell with the cracking phlegm in his throat and chest. He prattles without interruption until they reach the first floor and exit the building.

DaYana unbuttons her coat and reaches into the breast pocket to remove a pack of cigarettes and a lighter. She offers both to Dawkins.

"Aren't you going to smoke too?" he asks.

"I'm trying to quit."

"Ah, so am I," Dawkins says. He pulls a cigarette from the package, places it between his lips. He ignites the cigarette, breathes deeply, and exhales. "My current wife, she couldn't be much older than you. How old are you?"

Bouncing on the balls of her feet to generate heat, DaYana replies, "Twenty-five."

"Yes, a year younger than my wife. My new bride nonplussed my youngest daughter, who just turned thirty. However, my spouse makes me relatively happy and keeps me young. She sincerely worries about my health, and she nags me to stop drinking and smoking, but breaking bad habits is difficult for men of a certain age. When I was younger, everyone smoked, at least during social occasions. We were neither fully aware, nor particularly concerned with the physical or environmental impacts of our guilty pleasures. Did you know cigarette butts are not biodegradable? Huge environmental and economic burden."

"Yes," DaYana replies.

"It's quite terrible. My daughter gave me one of those e-cigarette devices for my birthday last year, but it isn't the same."

DaYana can feel the cold slicing her lips and slapping her bare skin.

"Maybe you can give me your thoughts on my writing right now, just a brief overview? Big things you noticed, and then we can talk more in-depth another time."

Dawkins stares up at the cloudy sky. When he eventually returns DaYana's gaze he says, "Yes, of course. But first, before I forget, I have two suggestions for you, if you'd really like to quit smoking. The first, chew cinnamon sticks. It helps sate the oral cravings, and it smells great. Number two, get yourself a boyfriend who will hold you accountable, Diana."

"My girlfriend usually makes sure I don't smoke. I'll look into the cinnamon sticks."

Dawkins' stare widens. "Oh, I apologize. I suppose looking at you, I should have guessed you were homosexual, right?"

DaYana bites her bottom lip, resisting the urge to rip the joking smirk from Dawkins' face.

"And about my writing?"

Dawkins readjusts his stance.

"Right, well…" And suddenly he is collapsing.

DaYana bends quickly to hook her arms around his torso, but his right knee clacks loudly against the icy sidewalk.

"Shit. Shit. Sir, are you okay?"

Dawkins turns his face away from DaYana's belly.

"Getting older is a series of indignities, Diana."

DaYana bears most of Dawkins' weight as he climbs back onto his feet. He pulls DaYana under his right arm. She becomes a crutch.

"Do you need to see a doctor? That sounded pretty bad."

"At my age, impacts like this are common. I only need to get off my legs for a while."

"Can you make it back upstairs?"

"I think it's best I retreat to my own quarters. We can talk there if you like, and I will undoubtedly need your aid trekking across the campus quad. My lodgings are accessible from the street, handi-capable, the president informed me, which I initially felt reluctant to accept but now am very grateful I did."

DaYana glances across the snowy lawn. She can see the lights of the faculty residence hall, but the expanse, glowing under floodlights perched at the edge of the building's façade, looks vast. In the quiet stillness, DaYana imagines that only she and Dawkins inhabit the entire campus.

She guides their first steps.

They wobble before finding a rhythm.

To the crunch of packed snow under feet and Dawkins' wheezing breath, DaYana lets her mind drift to her story...

...Leo's work ethic was what we had most admired. When the bells rang through the factory at 11 a.m., Leo often stayed behind at his station. We would return to the dormitories for lunch while he stood eating over a machine or a conveyor belt. Leo's hard work provided him opportunity to steal from the company, pocketing spare pieces, parts, and defective products for his selfish inventions. Dawkins tries to interject an anecdote about surviving Minnesota winters as a child and urinating his name into snow. DaYana ignores him. *Since Leo's death, we found many of his contraptions*

hoarded in the closet of his dormitory. Despite his work ethic, Leo never understood that a mature person might not always do what they want, but always what they must do. This may explain many of his peculiarities. He never sent money home to his family and never showed an interest in marrying. Leo didn't speak much, but when he did, he spoke of places he had never visited and destinations he longed to see.

And then DaYana is pushing though the door to Dawkins' residence. She is reaching intuitively for a light switch, flipping it on, and navigating Dawkins across the carpet. She seats him by the window on one of two matching wooden chairs parked beneath a half-circle kitchen table.

"Thank you," he says.

DaYana replies, "It's really late. I'm going to go back and go to bed. You should sleep too." She expels a final exasperated cough and turns to leave.

"But we haven't spoken about your writing yet."

"It's okay. Maybe tomorrow."

"No. I'm a man of my word. Look, Diana, do me a favor and go into the kitchenette over there. You'll find some plastic cups and a bottle of Speyside single malt Scotch, Aberlour 18. Pour one for yourself. You've earned it."

DaYana wants to tell him that she thinks he's had enough libations, but she complies. She returns to Dawkins with the half-empty bottle and two clear disposable cups. She pours him an inch and less for herself. Dawkins toasts his missing muse and takes a long sip.

DaYana follows. The alcohol warms her cold chest. She chokes at the taste.

"I first tasted Scotch when I was your age. My agent sent me a bottle after I signed the deal for my first novel."

"I didn't realize you were so young when you wrote *The Native Threat*."

"I presume you've read it."

"It's my favorite."

"Your favorite book I've written."

DaYana takes another sip from her glass and winces. "Actually, my favorite book, period."

"In our time together, I never perceived you to be an admirer of my work, Diana."

"I was really excited to join your workshop."

She avoids eye contact but can sense Dawkins' focus.

"I feel I've gotten to know you well, Diana, and I can be forth-coming with you. Based on your name and background, I can assume you are familiar with Charles Marlowe's *Tales of River*, and the work of Benjuan and Lupope."

DaYana squirms in her seat.

"Hemingway said, 'From all things that you know and all those you cannot know, you make something through your in-vention that is not a representation but a whole new thing truer than anything true and alive.'"

"Write what you know."

"Precisely! Readers are starved for ethnic stories, but why not write about your own people? It seems you would want to follow in that literary tradition, to speak on your people's experience."

"And what if I don't have anything to say about my people's experience?"

"Well, you surely have something to say about that perspective."

"Okay, what if I want to say something else, explore view-points beyond my own? Should I assume you've always written what you know? You have personal experience among warring colonies in distant galaxies?"

"You appear to be getting emotional. If you have been offended, that was not my intention. I'm only trying to give you sound advice. Like any industry, there are expectations. When it comes to writing and publishing, readers want to know that the author has authority. They might expect someone like me to write a literary science-fiction novel, whereas most readers would expect you to write about your own culture. I'm not saying it's right, but it's true. I didn't invent these expectations; they predate me. So, of course, when you decide to pen genre-bending short fiction featuring Chinese characters, it immediately raises questions about authenticity."

DaYana sucks her teeth.

"Diana, if you look at the most famous works of literary fiction, the books that become canon, they are firmly rooted in the author's own life experience."

DaYana gulps the rest of her Scotch. She clears her throat and says, "Fuck canon. I've never been a fan of classics. What about stories that defy convention? What about authors who challenge themselves to write about what they aren't familiar with in hopes of learning and sharing more about the world?"

"Plenty of authors try to inhabit another's skin through writing, and it most always fails."

"And that's a reason not to try?"

"You wanted to know how to improve your writing, how to be a successful author. That is why you are here. That is why you are talking to me. I'm telling you, as someone who has been at this for over three decades, a simple story based in your own personal experience is what to do. Play the race-culture-lifestyle cards you've been dealt. A gay, immigrant woman of color: that's a literary jackpot! You should be able to secure an agent with minimal effort if you just stick to the basics and write what you know."

"If I looked like you, would we even be having this conversation? I could pretty much write about whatever, wherever, whomever I wanted to and not have to worry about never getting published, right?"

"Yes. Again, I didn't set these precedents. But yes. I could write your story and it might be more widely embraced coming from me. However, I'm sure there would be some backlash from censor-happy social justice warriors online. If you do a

Chinese factory worker story, it is empathy. If I do it, it is cultural appropriation."

DaYana grins. "Must be difficult for you, knowing that if you fail in your portrayal of another group or race, you might have to hear their criticisms."

"But isn't that why you've grown so defensive, because I'm giving you criticism?"

"I don't think that's what this is."

Dawkins downs the rest of his drink. "Okay," he says, "your story's protagonist needs to have a clearer sense of longing. The narrator explains that—what's his name, Leo?—Leo likes to talk about places he's never seen, but that needs to be more specific. Where does he want to go? The reader needs to understand what attracts him to other places. Don't expect the reader to assume that Leo feels unfulfilled in his life and would be happier in another place. Why? That needs to be explained."

Dawkins pauses to belch and scratch his beard.

"And the voice of your narrator, Leo's comrade, needs to have more condemnation. Even if Leo were dead, the narrator would feel anger, even more so because Leo died irradiating himself with a machine that was bound to bomb. And there would definitely be consequences for the rest of the workers because of Leo's actions. The narrator's life would be upturned when the factory introduces stricter regulations. The narrator should sound at least a little inconvenienced. Change the tone, or switch to a distant third-person if you want more freedom in point of view."

Dawkins rocks softly in his seat.

"Thank you." DaYana says, nodding. "Seriously, that's all very helpful."

Dawkins tips his glass at DaYana for a refill. She pours, and he continues.

"I was like you. I think all beginning writers are like you. You want to defy expectations. You want to make something new, but readers don't like new, not really. Flannery O'Connor said, 'Endings have to be surprising but inevitable.' Like my last book, for example. It was predictable, nothing new, but clever enough to become a critical and commercial success. It met expectations. The truth is I can barely stand to do readings of that novel in public. However, I had a multi-book deal to fulfill and a family to support. At a certain point in every career, even yours if you stick with it, a storyteller must decide whether they intend to live on what they write. Once you've done that, you must then accept the fact that the unexpected doesn't sell."

Dawkins finishes the liquor in his glass. He reaches for the neck of the bottle. DaYana snatches the Scotch from the table and stands.

"You should sleep. So should I."

DaYana returns the Scotch to the kitchen and moves to exit the apartment.

"Perhaps you could stay for one more drink?"

"I'm tired. Maybe another time."

"I've enjoyed our intimate salon. You're decent company. Are you sure you have to leave?"

"Goodnight, sir." DaYana pulls open the door, and the cold rushes over her.

"Diana, what do you think happened to my missing muse?"

Turning around to face Dawkins, DaYana lingers in the doorway.

"I think she's somewhere sleeping," DaYana says.

Dawkins nods. "Did you read my last book?"

"I did. I've read all your books."

Dawkins' chest swells. "What did you think?"

"I thought you could have done better."

Dawkins leans back in his chair. He gazes up at the ceiling.

"Sometimes I feel like that opening line to Ellison's *Invisible Man*. I'm turning into some kind of phantasm. I'm vanishing, but when I try to sit down and write about it, I bore myself."

"Maybe you should try writing for other ghosts."

DaYana closes the door behind her as she leaves.

Outside, it has begun to snow.

She buries her hands in the pockets of her coat.

As she trudges across the campus to her residence hall, DaYana contemplates how to incorporate some of Dawkins' feedback. She thinks about his adamant recommendations and the basics of plot: a character, different but not unlike herself, moving from conscious into subconscious, from life to death to life again, on a journey from order to chaos to retrieve some great boon or personal insight. DaYana wonders if a good story can strive for innovation and still carry depth. She considers the possibility of defying convention and bending form and becoming successful without having to follow a restrictive template or parade herself as other.

Maybe, instead of dying predictably in a failed attempt to build a quantum teleportation device with pilfered microwave oven components, Leo succeeds in his experimentation.

Will this revision make Leo's story less authentic and therefore less marketable?

"Maybe," DaYana says to herself, "I won't be for sale."

Wind blows fat flakes of snow across her face. Squinting through the precipitation, DaYana can almost see Leo in his navy coveralls...*He stood beside an unkempt gravestone on a white hill overlooking building 6/20, the raw material processing center where he started working as a teenager after his parents had died.*

Seconds earlier, Leo had been tinkering with his device in the closet of his dormitory. An invisible hand had reached through his belly, gripped his spine, and pulled him forward through space to here, now.

For several minutes, kneeling in the snow to closely examine the columns on the headstone, Leo struggled to comprehend his own name etched in granite between the dates of his own birth and death. Rereading his home province on the top of the stone, Leo began to realize the significance of his invention. His mortality had never felt more apparent, yet irrelevant.

And DaYana, finally on her way to dream, grins too against the barren New England chill.

THE GHOSTS OF TAKAHIRO ŌKYO

Daisuke would find them in varying stages of decomposition, bleeding out into the snow or scattered over hiking trails, half eaten. Most would be hanging from the trees, the trunks so close and tight that in the perpetual twilight of Mount Fuji's shadow their limbs looked like strange branches sprouting from the shaggy moss. They were businessmen or star-crossed lovers, victims of incest, and criminals. They came from all over. It was not the books that inspired their deaths, Tsurumi's *The Complete Manual of Suicide* or *Kuroi Jukai* by Seichō Matsumoto. It was because of the yūrei. Many could not hear them—the sea of trees was as quiet as the depths of an ocean. But to Daisuke they were clear as his own voice, the forgotten words whispered in final breaths to the forest. Hundreds of confessions, the secrets kept by the undergrowth, were rooted in the soil and traveled the lengths of Japan like telephone wires—they called out to the lost and led them to Aokigahara.

Daisuke found them in much the same way, following the silent screams to the bodies of men and women who hoped that in death their souls might not be alone.

I

"Is it true?" Takahiro asks. He has been talking nervously for the last twenty minutes, but Daisuke has not been listening. This is their first walk-through together and they are less than a kilometer into the forest. Chief Yamamoto assigns new recruits to Daisuke because none of the others want to go out with him.

"Is what true?" Daisuke asks, grabbing the foam bill of his cap and pulling it lower. He savors the feel of the plastic mesh rubbing the bristles of his shaved head. The forest is so dense with trees that there is no wind, and in the summer, after hiking on patrol, his hair would mat against his forehead.

"The other forest workers, they call you..." Takahiro lowers his voice as if saying the words at a certain volume might conjure danger, "...a Shinigami."

Daisuke does not answer; he grunts in a way that means yes,

switching his gaze from the ground to the canopy. "How many bodies have you found?"

Of the forty-four corpses retrieved from the woods this year, Daisuke has discovered eighteen, the last six on consecutive patrols.

"Many," he says.

They come to a fork in the trail. Dividing the path is a large wooden sign that reads "Think calmly once again about them, your siblings and your children. Don't agonize over your problems—please seek counseling." Daisuke likes this sign. He wishes that he too could be a means of prevention. He wants to be one of the police officers patrolling around the forest. He has heard that they sometimes get letters from people they have saved. But he cannot be an officer because he has hemophilia and a chronic cough.

"Doesn't it bother you," Takahiro continues, "that the others call you a god of death?"

"We do not work for the dead," Daisuke reminds him. "We work for the living. Let's focus on that."

Takahiro shrugs, smooths his hair back, and replaces his hat onto his head. He is twenty-six, five years older than Daisuke, but his height and demeanor make him seem younger. In the forest, Daisuke is the elder, a veteran of Aokigahara, and he walks ahead of Takahiro in slow but purposeful strides. Occasionally he stops to look up. Much of the terrain looks the same, and due to a magnetic anomaly compasses do not work. It is easy to get lost, but Daisuke has learned to navigate by the crowns of the trees. The sun hits the tops of the leaves, and he charts the few beams of light breaking through the canopy like stars. Daisuke is confident he can always find his way back to the station, but he is frightened of being out in the woods after dark.

The path narrows into an incline that forces them to lean forward. They keep their hands in front of them in case they trip. It levels out, and then Daisuke hears it: a faint creaking. He turns toward the sound and scans the trees, trying to peer past the line of bark and into the darkness.

"There," he says to Takahiro, pointing. "Someone's out there."

Takahiro seems reluctant to leave the safety of the trail but follows Daisuke as he heads into the brush. Just a few yards from the path, a man wearing a suit begins to materialize. His back is facing them and he is looking to the ground.

Keep an eye out for abnormal behavior, the training manual suggests. *There are typically three kinds of visitors to Aokigahara: those interested in nature, those looking for a scare, and those with the intention of doing themselves harm. Pay attention to what they wear. Be mindful of people in business attire.* Daisuke grew up in Narusawa, one of the three villages that surround the forest. It was not abnormal to see taxis dropping off men from the train station in the early hours of the morning. They would reach into the breast pockets of their wrinkled suit jackets and remove rolls of bills. After handing the money to the drivers, they would stumble up into the forest, disappearing into the fog. Months, maybe years would pass before their bodies were recovered. When he was small, after he came to live with Chief Yamamoto, Daisuke would watch the forest workers carry the body bags into the station. If it was too late to take the corpse to one of the villages, they would drop it onto a bed in the spare room and janken to see who would have to spend the night lying beside a dead person. Sometimes, if the person guarding the corpse fell asleep or went to the bathroom, Daisuke would sneak into the room and unzip the bag. Sometimes he would find a man in a suit and run a curious finger along the collar, down to the buttons. Sometimes he thought he recognized them. Sometimes he would fall beside them in quiet sobs.

"Hello, sir?" Daisuke calls out. The man in the suit turns

around slowly, his head still trained at the ground. Daisuke starts to run. He wants so desperately to save something.

Takahiro yells after him, "Wait, hold on!"

But Daisuke puts more distance between them. He is a few feet from the man in the suit. He leaps over a fallen tree trunk, but the Earth vanishes beneath his feet. He plummets. Something ethereal says, "Kiyoshi Ishido." There is a wet pop, followed by a heavy crunch that bounces off the walls of his skull. The world is spinning now, leaves and dirt and thick branches in a washing machine. And then he is airborne again, only for a moment, before slamming onto his back. Daisuke's eyes fall shut. He lets his other senses provide context while he gathers the strength to rise. The soil under him is moist and has the tangy iron sourness of blood and bile. Something is dripping on his forehead, and he can hear Takahiro shouting out to him from somewhere above. When he finally looks up, there is the man in the suit, hanging above him, floating in a cloud of flies. Another drop falls from the tip of a dress shoe and onto Daisuke, rolling over his naked scalp. He twists his head slightly to the left.

Takahiro is at the top of the large hill, vomiting. He backs away from the drop-off, disappearing for a few minutes. When he returns, he wipes his mouth with the back of his hand.

"He's dead," Takahiro shouts down.

"I know," Daisuke barks.

"Are you okay?"

Daisuke hoists himself onto his elbows but keeps his eyes focused on the body above him, the swollen corpse with pale blue skin that complements the pinstripes of its suit. He rolls onto his stomach and pulls his knees under him. He knows the impact of the fall will have repercussions, the severities of which he can neither see nor fully imagine. Rising slowly to his feet, he hobbles forward only to collapse back onto the hard, wet ground. He is clutching his right ankle, and the toe of his boot is pointing down. Daisuke sprawls out on his back and reaches for his waist, where his radio would be. He sits up and searches the area. A short distance up the hill is his two-way, ripped perfectly in half.

"Takahiro, my ankle is broken, and so is my radio." Daisuke pauses to estimate the hill. "Call the station. Tell them we need two stretchers immediately."

Takahiro snatches his radio from his belt and presses the big black button. Something is wrong. The soft white-noise whoosh like television static is missing. Takahiro says, "Hello," but all that comes back is silence. Daisuke watches him fiddle with the knobs, frantic.

"The walkie-talkie is dead."

A minute passes before Daisuke finds the courage to suggest the only solution. "You're going to have to go back to the station."

"I can come down there and help you up."

"You can't carry me up this hill."

"We can try to find another way. We can follow the slope. It has to lead down to one of the villages, right?"

"Or we might get lost," Daisuke says.

Takahiro's legs are visibly shaking, but his voice is certain and dutiful. "I will run back to the path, try the radio again. If I don't get anyone, I will go back to the station and get help."

Okay, Daisuke thinks. He nods to Takahiro who turns to run, vanishing into the trees.

II

Chief Yamamoto could have done something other than work in Aokigahara. He was a strong student and a natural athlete. He could have been a businessman. But he had watched his father grow thin in suits, giving away pieces of himself as he tried to be what others needed him to be. Yamamoto could not drink away the afternoon he had discovered his father's body, dead at an office desk, clasping a pen, successful and alone, with a sneaky half-grin like he had a secret.

When the time came for him to head his father's ¥3 billion shoe company, he ran. He bought a ticket for an overnight bus, caught a train, and hailed a taxi to Mount Fuji, a place his father had always promised to take him but was always too busy to go. He watched white puffs roll off its snow-capped crown and waited to feel the mysticism he had anticipated as a boy. When he tired of its majesty, he started walking and discovered a small town at the base of the volcano called Narusawa. He rented a room at a lodge with the money he had left and applied for jobs in the area. He accepted the first offer, a position as a forest worker.

The work was easy and kept him fit. The worst part of the job was combing the forest once a year for bodies, but he approached it with a certain coldness that stemmed from the values his father had instilled in him: a strong skepticism of anything impractical and a will to win. He was far from superstitious. He did not believe in ghosts, and he could not change his competitive outlook. He imagined life as a kind of race against death. Those men and women he found in the forest were quitters. They had let death catch up to them and had surrendered to its speed. They were the losers, and that made Yamamoto a winner.

Years passed, and work in Aokigahara became less and less fulfilling. Yamamoto was given more responsibilities but never enough to satisfy his ambition or thirst for authority. He looked for other jobs, but finding work in Narusawa was difficult for an outsider, a fact of which his friend, Takahiro Ōkyo, seemed determined to remind him.

"Nobody is looking to hire some outsider from Kobe," Takahiro would say. "The only reason you found this job is because no one else would want it."

"You are okay with being a forest worker for the rest of your life?" Yamamoto would ask.

"Why wouldn't I? One should aspire only to their highest level of incompetence."

"You don't want things?"

"Of course I do. I want a roof over my head, heat in the winter, a fan in the summer, and a cold Sapporo every now and then.

This job affords me those things."

Eventually, Yamamoto subscribed to Takahiro's reasoning. He gave up trying to find another line of work, married a local girl from a nice family, rose to the title of deputy, and settled into the idea of retiring from Aokigahara with a pension. He started drinking on patrols with Takahiro, stumbling up and down the trails, debating everything, and cursing the spirits hiding amongst the trees. Then one day they wandered too far into the woods, and they saw the true nature of the Aokigahara. Confronted by a flaw in the laws of his existence, Yamamoto did what he did whenever he was truly afraid. He ran, leaving Takahiro behind to be swallowed by the forest.

Yamamoto went home to his wife. He did not return to the station for a week, hoping that time might correct itself and erase what he had seen. When people came looking for him, asking about Takahiro, he gave them a myth. He said that Takahiro had disappeared into the forest, and that was enough. After a few short months, Yamamoto's chief could no longer spare the money or the man hours to continue the search parties. Family, co-workers, the police, and curious strangers all seemed content to turn Takahiro into a tale like those they had known all their lives, proof of Aokigahara's terrible magic. But

Yamamoto never told the story enough times to believe it. He returned to work in the forest despite his wife's protests, hoping that he would find Takahiro waiting to forgive him.

III

Dusk settles around him, a violet hour, turning the humid heat of the forest frigid. Daisuke is beginning to slip in and out of consciousness. There is something oozing inside of him, and he knows that he will soon be dead. He is somewhat surprised by his own calm. Because of his condition, he has been close to dying. The circumstances of those near-death experiences were far less dramatic, and though the fear is still real, Daisuke is comforted by the fact that his life will not be ended by falling in the shower or coughing so hard he cracks a rib. In the last few minutes of sunlight, Daisuke finds acceptance, curiosity overshadowing his anxiety about what awaits him. He believes that at the very least his questions will be answered.

Daisuke plummets into darkness. He cannot tell if his eyes are open or closed. He listens for the drips from the body dangling above him, soft taps on the forest floor, but there is only silence, a void as vast and empty as the black. He hears the branch break, and the man in the suit falls with a violence that is more than just dead weight. The body lands on top of Daisuke, forcing the air out of his lungs and pinning him to the ground. He struggles to push the corpse off him, but his arms are noodles slapping against concrete. He tries to kick and wiggle himself out from under the man, but it only digs him deeper into the dirt. There is pressure behind his ears that spreads down the back of his neck and across his shoulders. He can feel capillaries burst. The weight is all around him now, crushing him.

Bubbling to the surface of his mind are memories that do not belong to him. Entire lives, worlds away, all of them sin and suffering. The floor of the forest turns to water and Daisuke is a small Dutch woman with bones like glass caught in the currents of the North Sea. Her legs cramp and she is pulled under, the dark blue crushing her chest like the beauty of the Kurhaus on the coast of Scheveningen. The salt water fills her lungs like fire, and Daisuke is a young Nigerian boy, burning in a Lagos pipeline explosion. His flesh sags and hardens, and he is a forgotten female civil rights hero freezing to death alone in her unheated rental house just four miles from the statehouse she helped diversify. And suddenly Daisuke is back in Aokiga-hara. He is Kiyoshi Ishido, the man in the suit, trudging into the forest, writing a note and tucking it into his breast pocket, pulling off his belt, climbing a tree, fastening the buckle around his neck. Daisuke is sliding off a thick branch, choking, thrashing, kicking, crying, and then he is still. As life drools out of him, he sees Takahiro standing on the hill, watching from below, folding his hat in his hands, mouthing something Daisuke knows is important. Something that looks like, "We are Takahiro Ōkyo."

IV

On the day my daughter was born, I held her in my arms, and I realized there was nothing I could offer her. I was an objective observer. I copied the behavior of others in an attempt to make my time more bearable. I thought if I pursued the things that others wanted, did the things that others did, if I worked hard and married young and had a baby, I would eventually feel a part of something. I never did. I never felt finished, and that sense of being incomplete prevented me from giving. I had no wisdom to share with her. No opinions. No lessons. I had nothing to share with anybody. Holding my daughter, I discovered that for the people I was supposed to love, all I had ever felt was obligation, a vague understanding of right and wrong. My life was a kind of déjà vu, a perpetual out-of-body experience marked by failed connections and intimate knowledge of places I had never been. Aokigahara always felt familiar to me. I had never visited the forest, but I knew I had been there. It called out to me. Standing in the sea of trees, looking for a place to die, those were the only moments of my existence, the only time everything did not look distant and transparent, like a copy of a real life reflected in a window. I could feel the energy traveling under my feet, reaching up into my veins, and it was the first time I ever felt tied to anything.

—Kiyoshi Ishido

V

Yamamoto received a call from his mother. She had hired a detective to find him, her son who had disappeared the day her husband was found dead in his office. He wept into the receiver. Yamamoto had not thought about his mother or the family he had abandoned. He had not called or made any other attempt to contact them, to offer his condolences, or to ease their fears. When his mother told him that his youngest sister was unmarried and pregnant, the weight of his betrayal seemed to fall down on him all at once. Yamamoto offered to take the baby because his body had failed to give his wife children, and because he thought by doing so he might atone for his absence.

The boy was born. Yamamoto traveled back to Kobe. His brother and mother made a point not to meet him at the hospital. Even his sister, pale and weak from birthing a bastard child, had a faint impression of disgust under her sleepy grin. Her eyes seemed sorrowful as she surrendered her baby to her coward of a brother. The boy went four days without a name until Yamamoto and his wife settled on Daisuke Matsuo, a name that would allow them to be open about his adoption and hide the identity of his real mother.

Daisuke was not a happy child, and from an early age he had a peculiar fascination with death. Yamamoto was unable to recognize that something was odd about the boy because he too was obsessed with death. Whenever his wife voiced her concerns—*the boy has no friends, he says he hears people talking even when no one is around, he suffers from night terrors, he draws nothing but black birds*—Yamamoto dismissed her. "Daisuke will find his own way," he would say. He was more concerned with the boy's poor physical health, a persistent cough and a medical condition that often caused him to bleed into his joints if he ran too fast. Yamamoto had hoped for a son with whom he could share his love of baseball and sports, but the boy did not have the ability or the constitution.

When Daisuke first asked to come with him to the station on one of his days off from elementary school, Yamamoto was more than happy to share his work with his son. He thought it was an indication of the boy's character, a sign of his initiative. However, Daisuke showed more interest in the forest than in scheduling patrols or making visitor brochures. He asked a lot of strange questions.

"Do you ever go out into the woods at night?"

"No. I've made a habit of making sure my men and I are back in the station by dusk."

"Is it true you find the bodies of people who kill themselves?"

"Sometimes, yes."

"Why do you think they do it?"

"I don't know."

"I think they do it because they are lonely."

"Maybe so."

Yamamoto's seniority and his appearance as a dedicated family man made him the clear choice to replace the chief in retirement. His promotion meant more hours at the station, and Daisuke dedicated more of his time to aiding his adoptive father, even volunteering to accompany him on overnight stays. By the time he was sixteen, Daisuke was a regular face among the men. Every afternoon he could be found studying forest maps, filing incident reports, or going on short patrols with Yamamoto.

"I want to work with you in the forest," Daisuke would say.

Yamamoto's reply was always the same. "Finish secondary school. Go to university, and then if you still want to work with me in Aokigahara, you can."

After graduating with a degree in physics, Daisuke returned to work at the station. Yamamoto, though a little apprehensive, kept his promise and hired his son. Yamamoto's wife was concerned that working in the forest would feed into the boy's obsessions and make it harder for him to be normal. She tried to encourage him to use his degree, to leave the village and Aokigahara. At dinner she would share gossip about interesting things happening in nearby cities. At breakfast she would read aloud from a newspaper, interjecting a job advertisement between every story.

It was not long after Daisuke started that other forest workers started coming to Yamamoto with complaints—*he says he hears voices, he says he would rather work alone, he is bad-tempered and rude*. "Daisuke will find his way," Yamamoto would say.

When Daisuke found his first dead body, everyone considered it a new recruit's bad luck. Recovering a corpse was a gruesome affair that involved hiking back to the station with a decomposing body strapped to a stretcher. It was difficult, physically and mentally. By the time Daisuke found his fourth, suspicions that he was looking for bodies started traveling around the station. By the sixth, Daisuke had earned the nickname Shinigami, a death god. It was getting harder for Yamamoto to ignore the fact that something was wrong. No one wanted to work with his son. The stories coming back to his office had the same key details—*Daisuke's neck twists, his eyes gloss over, he becomes unresponsive, he runs off into the woods, and there is a body*. What scared Yamamoto most was what his men refused to tell him. He had overheard them talking one night in the barracks about Daisuke and how, while running to a corpse, he would often scream a name. Sometimes those names matched some identification they would find on the body.

It continued. Daisuke started finding bodies more frequently. He shaved his head, and the effect was otherworldly. With his long, skinny limbs and big eyes, he looked like an alien. He stopped talking to his mother, and then he stopped talking to everyone. Yamamoto would not confront Daisuke or comment on his behavior because he was not prepared to find that he was partly responsible for his condition.

When Daisuke hobbled into the station, one of his feet turned completely around, pointing back the way he came, his clothes soaked through with blood and sweat, dragging a body by the neck with an Italian leather belt, screaming a hundred names, one of them a forest worker who died over twenty years ago, it was the first time Yamamoto had been genuinely afraid since he had last seen Takahiro.

In that moment, watching Daisuke's wild eyes trying to escape his head, two of Yamamoto's worst fears were realized. The first, that he was mentally ill and could somehow pass his sickness on to Daisuke, and the second, that what he had seen in the forest all those years ago was real and Daisuke had seen it too. He had been unfair, raising him so close to the forest—*a child has no place around so much death.* His wife had told him that. She was scared that the lonely yūrei might follow the boy home.

Daisuke dropped the belt. He dropped a single sheet of blood-stained paper, most likely a suicide note. He collapsed to the floor beside the corpse and began shouting the name Takahiro Ōkyo.

Yamamoto knew then that he had failed Daisuke. Yamamoto knew it was his own fault for running away, for giving up his search so that the weight of his redemption fell upon his son, his fault for coming to Aokigahara in the first place, for refusing to leave just because he had stayed so long, for not knowing who he was if he was not Chief Yamamoto.

VI

Daisuke wakes to the smell of antiseptic and sterilized linoleum. Behind the buzz of fluorescent lights, he can make out the sound of the universe expanding. He is in a hospital bed, and his right foot is missing. Chief Yamamoto stands above him, looking stern and impatient. Daisuke smiles weakly, his body heavy with the weight of his new consciousness. He understands things now, the thin line between superstition and science, re-incarnation, large concepts with many syllables, time dilation, and the relativity of simultaneity. No moment is absolute, and energy can neither be created nor destroyed. He was, is, and will be Takahiro Ōkyo and Daisuke Matsuo and Kiyoshi Ishido and over half a dozen other people throughout space and time.

Chief Yamamoto clears his throat. "What happened?"

Daisuke knows what happened. He has seen the mechanisms of God.

"I went out into the forest," Daisuke says.

"You were not scheduled to be on patrol."

"I know that now."

"Why did you go out alone?"

Daisuke sighs as if he has been asked to explain something simple. "I was lured out into the forest by Takahiro Ōkyo."

Chief Yamamoto eyes him curiously. He buries his nose in the palms of his paper hands, breathes deeply, and rubs his face. "Takahiro died over twenty years ago. How do you know that name? You never met him."

Staring at the end of the bed, at the void across from the

toes pointing up through the linens, Daisuke asks, "Why do you make one of the men in the station sleep beside the bodies you find in the forest?"

Chief Yamamoto fails to hide his surprise. His mouth hangs open while he searches for context.

"Why are you asking?"

"You do not believe in yūrei."

"No, but my men do. I don't need them worrying about dead people walking through the barracks or screaming through the night, so someone has to lie with the corpses."

"Their fears are no less valid than yours. They all stem from how little we understand death. Whether it is spirits or becoming our father, it all leads back to death."

"I did not say..."

"That is what you are afraid of, isn't it? That if you become like your father, you might have to die too?"

Chief Yamamoto tries to scoff, but he is choked by his own fear. He manages to summon a tone of condescension he reserves for new recruits to the forest station. "You seem so certain."

"Yes, because you told Takahiro, and he told me."

"Takahiro is dead." Beads of sweat are running down Chief Yamamoto's temples now.

Daisuke nods, knowingly. "And still I met him. Even though you left him writhing in the dirt with a broken spine, I know him." Chief Yamamoto stands pencil straight, his eyes darting from side to side, scanning over something invisible. Daisuke imagines it is a list of possible scenarios—Takahiro's name was used in passing or written out on old employment documents. "Your father passed naturally, and he met death unafraid," Daisuke says. "There was nothing natural about Takahiro's death. He smashed his own head with a rock to escape the pain. He never got to understand and accept it. He knew death only as an alternative to suffering."

Chief Yamamoto shakes his head. "You could not know that...this would have happened before you were born."

"I wasn't born yet, but a part of me was there."

"That is impossible."

But Daisuke knows Chief Yamamoto can feel something shift in the room, reality bending the rules around them, the world reshaping into a place where the things Daisuke suggests are possible. "I went back for him. I kept looking. I wanted to give him a proper funeral. I at least wanted to put his soul to rest."

But there is no absolute state of rest. A man kills himself. He is punished. His soul is divided, twenty-six cuts for every year of his life, and those pieces of himself take on entirely new lives, lives spent trying to remedy that division, to fill that void.

"I could not find him," Chief Yamamoto says. His eyes gloss over with regret, but his voice is steady with truth. "I never stopped looking."

But time and the distribution of energy are relative. More than a dozen people, sharing the same soul, each carrying an internal clock of identical design and function, moving in motion relative to each other and situated differently in regard to varying gravitational masses, will always view those other clocks as wrong. The death of Takahiro Ōkyo is simultaneous with Daisuke's conception, but it occurs later in the lives of Sarah Bal and Reginald Halpert, and precedes the birth of Adekunle Ogunleye and Becca Rubinstein. They are not parallel worlds, just events occurring in different order all dependent on the motion of the observer.

"What did you see in those woods that day?" Daisuke asks. "What made you so afraid?"

"We were on patrol in the forest." Chief Yamamoto swallows hard. He fights to finish, as if by getting it out he might absolve himself. "We were drinking rice wine out of our canteens. We had left the hiking trails for some reason. I think Takahiro said he had found a shortcut, but he hadn't. We got lost. We thought as long as we followed the slopes down we would find our way out. When we saw the end of the trees, we thought we had made it to one of the villages, but it was a caldera, the hills of Aokigahara rolling down into a smooth basin of volcanic rock, like a navel. And suddenly the ground started shaking. It was so violent, so close, right under our feet. I thought Fuji was erupting, but it wasn't. The Earth opened up right in front of us, and something big and dark flew out. We started running back into the forest. I could hear Takahiro's feet pounding behind me and, behind him, something heavy ripping through the trees. Then he screamed, and I could not hear his feet anymore. I kept running. I was too scared to turn around. When I finally looked over my shoulder, I saw him folded in half, crushed in the talons of a giant black crane."

"You saw death," Daisuke says, grinning like he's proven something no one knew to be true.

Chief Yamamoto moves closer to the bed. His brow falls and wrinkles from his new comprehension. He leans forward until

Daisuke can feel his breath and his anger. "What are you?"

Daisuke searches Chief Yamamoto's tiny pupils for a sign of fear but is comforted to see none, only a reflection of himself propped up in the hospital bed. There was a time when they would have been too afraid to look into the darkness and have it stare back at them. They are beyond that now—they've moved past it together. Daisuke closes his eyes. He listens to the ticking of his heart and imagines the churning of cosmic cogs pushing him into another second.

ACKNOWLEDGMENTS

"They Would Be Waiting," *J Journal*; "Memorial," *Auburn Avenue*; "Lalita Rattapong's New Microwave," *Metazen*; "Preface to *Tales of River*," *Knee-Jerk Magazine*; "She Is a Cosmos," *Inscape*; "Takeaway," *Cleaver Magazine*; "(No Subject)," *Queen Mob's Teahouse;* "Twin Pilgrims," *Puerto del Sol;* "A Selfish Invention," *Storychord;* "The Ghosts of Takahiro Ōkyo," *Hunger Mountain*.

Many thanks to the friends and editors who saw earlier versions of these pieces:

Rigoberto González, Trinie Dalton, Domenic Stansberry, Jess Row, Douglas Glover, Adam Berlin, Jeffrey Heiman, Chuck Huru, Christopher Allen, Amanda Cal Louise Phoenix, Karen Rile, P.E. Garcia, Brandon Taylor, Lakiesha Carr, Tyrese L. Coleman, Ngwah-Mbo Nana Nkweti, Jeni McFarland, David Haynes, Naima Yael Tokunow, Kate Senecal, Gish Jen, Miciah Bay Gault, Barry Wightman, Erin Elizabeth Smith, Panasit C., Tatiana Ryckman, Emily Roberts, LK James, Wendy M. Walker, and Kima Jones.

With love to Bailey Gaylin Moore.

I'm very grateful for the continued support from Tim Antonides, Jason Arment, Gayle Baldwin, Alexa Bartel, Al Black, Mike Blair, Ian Bodkin, Nicole Brown, Conleth Buckley, Catherine Buni, Mathieu Cailler, Tobias Carroll, Colin Cheney & Anna Brown, Jennifer Cohen, Lydia Cole, Louise Crowley, Cathleen Cuppett, Kristie Frederick Daugherty, Jesse Dávila, Tara Dempsey, Celeste Doaks, Madeleine Dubus, Mary Catherine Farrell, Courtney Ford, John Foster, Arlia Frink, Roxane Gay, Andrea S. Gilham, Peter J. Gloviczki, Christina Gustin, Casey Hancock, Jane Poirier Hart, Hopeton Hay, Jennifer Heisel, Nick Hilbourn, Greg Hill, Mandy Holland, Adam & Landon Houle, Corinne Jenkinson, Justin Johnson, Karen Kelly, Jacqueline Kharouf, Susan King, Rhoda Knight, Anu Kumar, Diane Lefer, George Lellis, Sunisa Manning, Robert McCready, Josh Michael, Damien Miles-Paulson, Aisha Moorer, Tomás Q. Morín, Mai Nardone, Mel Pennington, John Proctor, Richard Puffer, Erin Record, Laura Reed, Victorio Reyes, Mary Rickert, Stephanie Rizzo, Nicolas Leon Ruiz, Elizabeth Schmul, Rion Amilcar Scott, Sophfronia Scott, Sarah Seltzer, James Bernard Short, Javier Starks, Breana Steele, John Taylor Stout, Cheryl Telligman, Lee Thomas, Rachel Thompson, Cedric Tillman, Kali VanBaale, Ian Wallace, Michael Waskom, Graham Wood, Ben Woodard,

Cheryl Wright-Watkins, Sara Wyatt-Witherspoon, Natalie M. Zeigler, and Pam Zhang.

Much love to my family: Dorothy Quist, Hammond J. Quist Jr., Dr. Faustina Quist, Sena Quist, Selorm Quist, Charlie Van Ngo, Kunsiri, Vichit, and Pitchsinee Jiratra-Anant.

With endless gratitude to the places that provided me the time and space to do this work: Charles W. and Joan S. Coker Library-Information Technology Center, Vermont College of Fine Arts, Assumption University of Thailand, Kimbilio Fiction, and Sundress Academy for the Arts.

In memory of Rev. John Foster III

Donald Quist is the author of the nonfiction collection *Harbors* (Awst Press). Find him online at donaldquist.com

AWST
PRESS

"The words gathered into a book of fiction are often said to conjure up a world. Usually this is an exaggeration, but what Donald Quist has accomplished in *For Other Ghosts* is to truly give us what feels like an entire world›s breadth and depth. The range, sensitivity, and brilliance of these stories are astounding. His readers are in for a mind-expanding experience."

—Jamel Brinkley, author of *A Lucky Man*

"Elliptical, unconventional, tense, and beautiful, the stories in *For Other Ghosts* will haunt you. In his essays, and now in his fiction, Donald Quist has made it clear that he's a writer to watch."

—Martha Southgate, author of
Third Girl from the Left and *The Taste of Salt*

"I read *For Other Ghosts* with an increasing awe, my world expanding with each sentence. And that›s what Donald Quist›s writing does, enlarges your world as it enlivens it, making you aware of your connection to the things and people around you. This is a book written with passion and sensitivity for all that's human in us."

- Rion Amilcar Scott, author of *Insurrections: Stories*

"Donald Quist is a master of the unspoken, the way the heaviness of loss, conviction, and fear can both alter a life and haunt it. *For Other Ghosts* is a beautifully crafted collection that will make you question many things and illuminate many more."

—Natalia Sylvester, author of
Everyone Knows You Go Home and *Chasing the Sun*

"*For Other Ghosts* sweeps across a globe interlinked and imperiled as never before by technology and industrialization, and hits pause only to gaze unflinchingly into how the individual smacks against the most unexpected of impediments. What kind of justice is to be found in these troubled times? How do we navigate the inescapable imprint of US empire—as insiders, as outsiders, here and abroad? These are the momentous questions that Quist courageously and graciously pursues, his prose precisely chosen and evocative, his range of deftly crafted characters authentic and indispensable."

—Vanessa Blakeslee, author of
Perfect Conditions: Stories, Juventud, and *Train Shots*